THE NIGHT
WATCHMAN

Dedicated to Rosemary Morris
for her professional help and guidance.

© Michael Kelly 2011
Published by McIntyre Press, Liverpool
Book design by March Design, Liverpool
Printed by Martins the Printers, Berwick

ISBN 978-0-9568414-0-7

Acknowledgements

In writing this book of short stories I find that there are many people who
I wish to thank. Firstly, I would like to thank my editor Rosemary Morris
for her great patience and Lyn Adams for reading and correcting my
grammar, also Angela Mounsey for her invaluable help and use of the
cover photograph. With special thanks to Sarah Hughes for her wonderful
support and encouragement. Mr. Ryan, my school teacher, who influenced
my thinking about music and story telling. Margaret Graham and Anne
Davies for their wonderful friendship and encouragement. Also Marie
McDaid who is always there when I need literary advice.
I must thank David Charters, columnist with the *Liverpool Daily Post*, for
his wonderful support and encouragement. Also Linda McDermott for
highlighting my work on her late night programme BBC Radio
Merseyside. Roger Phillips for my interview on BBC Radio Merseyside on
my first edition of *The Life and Times of Kitty Wilkinson* back in 2000.

www.mikekellybooks@gmail.com

Also by Michael Kelly
Merseyside Tales
The Life and Times of Kitty Wilkinson
Liverpool's Irish Connection
Mothers of the City

THE NIGHT WATCHMAN

And Other Stories

Michael Kelly

McINTYRE PRESS

CONTENTS

FOREWORD

Broad of shoulder, dandy of step, the man stares at you from behind the thick lenses of his glasses and there is a quizzical smile in the blue of his eyes, which seems to anticipate pleasure in your company. Yes, Mike Kelly is a sociable fellow, the wearer of a fine cap of Donegal tweed and the teller of stories – both true ones and those stretched a little to fit the circumstances and his own fancy. In this latest volume, Mike, who has already written history books and biographies, returns to his first love of fiction. Although a Liverpudlian by birth, the mood of his ancestral Ireland is all around him, his manner squeezed from the auld peat. In the tradition of James Joyce and Brendan Behan, Mike writes of the street people with compassion and humour. I am glad to call him a friend.

David Charters
Feature writer and columnist, *Liverpool Daily Post*

PREFACE

The stories I have narrated in this volume are, in the main, about an age gone by. They tell of a time and people who have almost disappeared, at least the circumstances in which they lived. My stories are about people I grew up with, they were mainly of Celtic stock, Irish, Welsh, and Scots together with the English, who made up the majority of the population at that time. They blended together to form my view of the world.

Many of the stories have a humorous or funny side to them but they also recall sadness, nostalgic and a simply way of life. In the main they are the lives of people who worked on the docks, in the factories or those who hoped to seek adventure by joining the Merchant Service in times of war and peace.

They were as happy with their lives as those who lived and worked in better circumstances, away from the smells and sounds of the docks and factories. They were good, decent people who were satisfied with their station in life. The Liverpool of today is changed and in many ways for the better for most. We can still smile even when some emphasize the wrong side of our character.

In recent years we have seen the folk from other distant lands coming to live amongst us. The new Liverpudlians bring the richness of their cultures, all adding to the wonderful fabric of our lives.

THE NIGHT WATCHMAN

Jimmy McIntyre's duties consisted of walking up and down the ship's deck but never going out of sight of the gangway. He was the night watchman, and looked a very sad figure, in his dark overcoat, which hung insecurely from frail shoulders and reached down to his ankles. It could easily have fallen like an empty sack to lie at his feet, exposing his body to the wind. His eyes were downcast, and the slow movement of his legs portrayed weariness as he walked the ship's deck.

Jimmy, at the age of fifty-two, was a physical wreck. His stomach had been cut away by the surgeon's knife, his sea days were over and this was how he would spend what little time he had left on this earth – not much of a reward for a lifetime of hard and bitter work at sea.

At the age of thirteen he left St. Alexander's School, Kirkdale, Liverpool, having exhausted the curriculum. He was a good and intelligent pupil, and the best copperplate writer, but his parents could not afford to keep him at school. Poverty and low wages coming into his family home leaned his thoughts to romantic ideas of seafaring.

He had to wait until he was seventeen, a further four years, before he could join a ship. Jimmy's feelings for the sea did not diminish during the waiting years, as the sea was all around him. Every day, as he walked onto the docks, he would see ships of all nations entering and leaving the port, and some tied up at the quayside unloading cargoes from foreign countries.

He would watch in envy as the young seamen passed him along the quay after embarking from a newly arrived ship. 'One day that will be me being paid off from a ship with plenty of money in my pocket,' he thought. Jimmy's young mind would be full of adventures, thinking of the day that would come when he would be somebody in the street where he lived. Time passes very slowly when you are sixteen longing to be seventeen. He could hardly contain himself as he waited for the wonderful day when he would be able to go to the shipping office to sign on for his first ship, and sample the great adventures that surely lay ahead. In the meantime, however, he was to toil during the long summer days and dreary dark hours of winter with the ship repair men, sometimes being laid off for a couple of weeks at a time because the work was only casual.

Despite some of the older hands in the gang that Jimmy worked with, trying to persuade him not to make his life the sea, he never wavered for an instant, so taken up with his dreams was he.

"It's all work and no pay, and the food is lousy. It's no life if you get married," said one of his workmates. Jimmy had listened to all the reasons as to why he should change his mind but he was steadfast.

It was now time to make contact with the right people for the advice he needed. Jimmy's father was a seaman, not that Jimmy had seen much of him, as he was always away or stranded in some South American port after missing his ship because he was drunk. This meant his mother had her allowance (the portion of a seaman's pay that was handed to his named next of kin by the Shipping Company) stopped. When this happened, for any reason, it was a big problem finding enough money to feed the family.

This was the background, which helped shape Jimmy's future plans, as he made his way to the shipping office of the company his father and elder brother had sailed for.

"So you want to go away to sea and be a stoker?" said the Shipping Master, looking up in amusement, through the little reading glasses perched on the end of his nose, at Jimmy, who wondered if he was about to be rejected.

"Well, you will have to do dirty work if you want to be a stoker," he continued, still looking up at Jimmy, "and you will have to be a hard man. How old are ye, seventeen? They're all hard men you know, you'll be sailing with very tough, hard men." The Shipping Master looked straight into Jimmy's eyes. "Well, if it's the sea you want we'll see what we can do for you. We'll let you know."

So Jimmy left with a smile and joyous heart to await his call to the sea. He joined his first ship in Huskisson Dock, Liverpool, on a cold November day in 1917. It would take him away from a land fit for heroes. The only things Jimmy had known during his young days in Liverpool were misery and poverty. But now this fine, good looking, budding sailor, with fair hair and blue eyes, slim frame and strong shoulders, was leaving the port of Liverpool for distant, and to him at that time, enchanted lands far away.

The only excitement that Jimmy McIntyre would get from his sea voyages would be the few hours spent alongside the docks in foreign lands. Most of the time would be a living hell for him and his shipmates below in the stokehold, but there were some good times ashore with the lads, doing the sorts of things you could never tell your family about. The steam ships that ploughed around the world's oceans were hungry beasts made of steel. Their bellies had to be fed with coal twenty-four hours a day, by young men also made of steel to match their charges.

Over the years Jimmy was to sail in many ships, even in a couple of Yankee boats, mostly on what was known as the 'Coffee Run' to South America. His first few trips down below in the boiler room were in front of the furnace, working as a trimmer, pushing the coal forward for the experienced fireman. The fireman would knock up the latch on the furnace door with his shovel, then lift a load full of coal, swing it round to face the furnace and throw it about five feet into the boiler; an action which took a lot of strength and skill, even from an experienced man.

Stokers wore heavy boots to protect their feet from the hot steel plates that they stood on. These also helped them keep their balance when they pitched the coal into the furnace. A ship's fireman could always be recognized, even years after his sea days were over, because his leather belt would be fastened at the back; an old custom from days gone by, to stop the buckle from getting too hot from the open furnace, and also to stop it digging into his stomach every time he bent to pick up a shovel of coal to pitch into the mouth of the monster.

Naval captains could majestically sail the seven seas, yachtsmen could fight nature, and each perhaps would get a little closer to God, but the ship's stoker would always be nearer to the devil. Sailing ships and yachts had sails to catch the wind to move them across the oceans, and they were only a fraction of the size of a steamer. All the energy that was needed to move those massive steam ships, through fair seas and gale force winds, depended entirely on young men like Jimmy McIntyre. Without them the monster furnace would stand there cold and empty, the pistons motionless, the engine useless, and the shaft and propeller gathering barnacles. The steam ship had young men of iron buried deep within its bowels who shovelled continuously to feed its belly with coal, which in turn made the steam to move the giant pistons that would drive the ship's engines and make the propeller turn, forcing the steamer across the seas.

The inevitable fate of most of Jimmy's shipmates would be death before the age of sixty, with the constant heat shrivelling the fluid from their bodies each time they went on watch. Four hours was a long time to spend in the boiler room, sweating and consuming many pints of non-too clean water. The watch over, they then climbed out of the stokehold onto the open deck, sometimes to be greeted by the rays of the sun and a soft breeze. At other times, the chilling gale-force winds would tear into their sweat-covered bodies, as they walked along an uneven deck to the fo'csle head, to rest in primitive conditions which only added to their misery.

It was almost a miracle that any man would continue to subject himself to such a life, but Jimmy's shipmates were modest men who would praise the ship that could get a good head of steam, and one that would not demand too much from the energy in their solid muscles. Day and night the ship's engines would need attention to keep them in good condition; and every year or two the ship would go into dry dock for a clean up and general inspection to make sure she was in a good order.

The stoker would also be given a brief, periodic inspection by a non-too concerned doctor, to see if his heart was still in moderate working order, and if he still had the strength to allow him to carry out the function required. Otherwise, he too would be cast to one side like an old sack. This was the life Jimmy McIntyre had chosen and he would work among some of the strongest and toughest men he would ever meet; in time he too became one of them.

During his sea days he was used to taking over the watch at four until eight o'clock in the morning; four hours on and four off throughout his voyages. The man taking over would always have a quick look in front of the boiler to make sure that the stoker he had relieved had left enough coal to get started. If not, there would be a few snide remarks made before he climbed up the steel ladder to the fiddley (the steel deck above the boiler or engine room) to collect his washing, which would be dry in no time at all from the heat rising from the boilers.

Jimmy always checked the Pearson's water-level gauge, then a quick look at the steam pressure. Sometimes the second engineer would also check, then go on his way when he was sure everything was shipshape.

Food was never plentiful at sea and Jimmy recalled going up to the galley in the hope that he could get the cook to part with a piece of raw meat in exchange for some tobacco. If Jimmy and the rest of the watch were lucky, the cook would cut a large joint of meat and hand it to him.

"Here," the cook would say, "go and throw that into the furnace and don't come back or ya will get me the sack."

Jimmy would then have a smile on his face as he descended the steel ladder from the fiddley down to the boiler room, where the rest of the gang would be waiting in anticipation. When Jimmy produced his prize, their smiles would be brighter than the fire in the furnace. Out would come the special coal shovel that was always kept clean and shiny enough to act as a mirror. Every man would be excited at seeing the meat put into the furnace. A few minutes later they pulled out the 'black pan', cooked to the liking of every man in the stokehold.

A terrible screech brought Jimmy's thoughts back to the present. He pulled the collar of his overcoat tight around his neck and looked over the side of the ship to see two cats down on the quay screeching at one another; their green eyes shining in the half-light from the lamps on the dock shed. A confrontation was going on between the adversaries, which broke the quietness and the loneliness of the night for Jimmy. 'These two cats could have been two stokers having a disagreement,' he thought.

The ship on which Jimmy was now a watchman was a lot different from the coal burners he had sailed on; this one was oil-fired and the boiler room was clean, with no loose coal underfoot to break a man's ankle. Conditions on board ships were so different, not at all as it was in days gone by.

After a quick look over the side of the ship to make sure no one was about, Jimmy slipped into the fiddley to warm his frail body. At about midnight, after making sure the coast was clear, he would make his way to the galley where he was certain to get something to eat from the cook. If he was no longer there, then the cook would have left him something to help drive the cold from his body. Jimmy got to thinking about how he was the only one to stay friendly with cooks in his seagoing days; and here he was still keeping in with one after those days were over. The cook had gone to bed, leaving Jimmy to lock the galley door when he had finished his snack.

As Jimmy McIntyre sat in the warmth of the galley enjoying his beef sandwich and keeping his hands warm around his mug of tea, his mind drifted once again, back through the years which had gone by so quickly. He remembered how they would clean out the ashes from under the furnace, pulling them out with the steel rake, then shovelling them into the forty-five gallon oil drums that stood on the steel plates. Once full, a member of the crew would climb the ladder to the top of the boiler room, and send the winch cable down to hook onto the oil drums. With their contents of ashes they would be winched up to the top, then taken on deck where they would be dumped over the side of the ship. 'Well, it could have been worse,' he thought, 'at least I did see different aspects of life abroad.'

It was cold and damp outside on deck, but Jimmy was not the sort of man to sit around too long, so he soon got to his feet, and stepped over the 'combing' (raised step) as he went through the doorway onto the deck. He made his way to the gangway, where he looked over the side to see the same two wild cats still going at it hammer and tongs.

Jimmy McIntyre smiled. 'Not a worry in the world,' he thought. 'Yet even they find something to fight over. One thing about them, they keep the rat population down. Without the wild cats the rats would take over.'

At four o'clock, the sound of a taxi pulling up at the

gangway broke the now silent night. A young deck officer walked onto the gangway leading a young woman down to the waiting vehicle. 'Some things never change,' thought Jimmy.

The night drew on, as he stood on deck looking up into the clear sky with not a cloud about. Jimmy smiled and thought aloud. "It's like a beautiful stage with the curtains drawn back to show the flickering lights of the stars; such a vast expanse." The sound of another taxi coming to a halt at the bottom of the gangway brought Jimmy's eyes down again. Three crew-members alighted from the cab to walk up, like silent players across the stage, oblivious of Jimmy's presence. 'A ship never sleeps,' Jimmy thought as he watched them, 'it's always got one eye open.'

The long night was almost over as the light of a raw November day pushed its way through on the horizon. Jimmy McIntyre signed the time-book at the top of the gangway, bringing an end to his twelve-hour shift.

The cold air was still reverberating around Jimmy's neck as he pulled his collar tight and turned to step onto the gangway. A small dark object came into contact with his foot and, looking down, he could see two bright eyes and just hear a faint sound. Jimmy picked the kitten up and looked at it. "A wild cat you may be," he said, pushing the kitten inside his overcoat, "but you and me are going to be shipmates." With the kitten warm against his chest, he wandered down the road to the room he occupied in the large old house in North Liverpool. He could not help but think that, at the end of a hard working life, all he ended up with was living in a single room, with only the newly found semi-wild cat as his best friend.

A PAIR OF SHINING BOOTS

Joe sat on the side of his bunk, listening to the rest of the young National Service recruits all chatting away. They all appeared a bit nervous in their new surroundings. Most of the young eighteen and nineteen year olds were trying to put a shine on their new army boots; just one of the first steps they had to learn in taking care of themselves. Joe smiled to himself as he looked down at the black pair of boots perched on his lap. His smile turned into a grin, and his head started to go up and down as though controlled by a spring, his young mind searching as it brushed away the years to the days when he was eleven years old.

The boots were the same, but much smaller. Joe could still remember the day when he arrived at 'Martin's Camp' during the war years. He alighted from the bus with dozens of other boys, a tag tied to his lapel displaying his name, age and religion. As Joe had walked through the gateway a sign over a small building had the words "All personnel and visitors report here," but there was no sign of life inside the building. Most of the lads tried to look into the windows, as they were hurried along.

After going only a few yards into the Camp the boys had been brought to a halt by a kindly looking man who seemed quite old to Joe and the rest of them. Their ages ranged between ten and fourteen and this man would become known as Daddy Rimmer to all who finished up in his class, although this place was not a school. The boys had already started talking about their surroundings within minutes of arriving.

"This is an army camp," they kept repeating to one another.

"Yes, I've seen army camps on the flicks," said one of the older boys.

"So have I," added a little ten-year-old.

"Right lads, line up in twos," said Mr. Rimmer. "When you are all ready, follow me."

Joe and his young comrades were led away to the dining room, clutching the few possessions they had. Joe listened to the sound of the birds that filled the air, and looked up trying to detect their whereabouts. He saw birds of all shapes and sizes, some sweeping low above the marching boys, then climbing high into the sky with such speed that the naked eye could hardly follow. Joe would have liked to have been able to name the beautiful birds, but none had filled the skies in the war-torn Liverpool he had just left behind.

As Joe and the rest of the boys entered the dining room he could see three men standing at the far end.

"All come to the front and sit down at the tables," said the taller of the men.

Once seated, all the boys were given a glass of milk.

"While you are drinking I would like to introduce myself. I am your Headmaster, Mr. Roach and this is Mr. Davies and Mr. Rimmer, who you will get to know in the days to come. Well boys, I would like to welcome you all to Martin's Camp, and I hope you enjoy your being with us here in the Cheshire countryside."

So began their stay and for most of them it was a pleasant experience.

"Come on, Scouse, get on with cleaning your boots, you look like you're day dreaming, thinking about home are you?"

"No," said the startled Joe as he saw the fresh-faced young man sitting facing him. "I was in a place like this when I was only eleven."

"You must be mad," said the young man. "You were

in an army camp when you were eleven?"

"Yes, all the boys were between ten and fourteen and we were evacuees from Bootle."

"Where is Boot-hill?" said the young man with a Somerset accent.

"It's part of Liverpool and its not Boot-hill, it's Bootle," replied Joe.

"I see, so you're from Bootle."

"Yes, but it's Liverpool," continued Joe.

The young man went silent for a few seconds. "My name's Jimmy Adams, what's yours?"

"Joe O'Neill."

"Did you really get evacuated to an 'Army Camp' or are you just kidding me?" Jimmy questioned.

"Yes, I'm telling the truth, and we had 'pee the beds'," said Joe.

"'Pee the beds'?" said Jimmy with a smile, "what do you mean 'pee the beds'?"

"Well, when we were kids we all had to sleep in bunks, and if you peed the bed you had to sleep on the bottom bunk, so that way the lad on the bottom bunk would not get wet," explained Joe.

"What happened if a lad did pee the bed? Would he be punished for it?" said Jimmy.

"No, but he had to drag his mattress outside of the billet to dry it out," smiled Joe.

"It must have been a right funny sight seeing all those wet mattresses drying outside;" laughed Jimmy, finding the whole thing very amusing.

"It never lasted very long."

"What never lasted very long?" asked Jimmy.

"The lads wetting their beds," Joe replied.

"Well how did they stop it?"

"They didn't get any milk going to bed," said Joe.

Jimmy looked at him waiting for further explanation.

"Every night we would march into the dining room for our supper. Every lad knew the place where he had to sit at the long rows of tables running the full length of the dining room. After being told to stand easy, you took your seat and in front of you on the table was a piece of fruit cake and a glass of milk, but in front of the 'pee the beds' there was only a piece of cake but no milk."

Jimmy looked on in amusement at what Joe was saying. "How many lads were in your camp?"

"About two hundred," said Joe.

"Two hundred lads," said the startled Jimmy, "and were you one of the 'pee the beds'?"

"No I was not, do you think I would be telling you if I was one?"

"Why not, all young lads pee the bed sometime or other."

"I suppose you're right but I was not one of the 'pee the beds' in the camp."

"Sure you're not having me on about this 'Martin's Camp', Joe?"

"No Jimmy, I'm telling the truth."

"What was the camp like?"

"It was like this one except that it had bunk beds," continued Joe.

"Yes, but it also had 'pee the beds'," said Jimmy with a grin that spread across his round face. "Do you think there might be a few 'pee the beds' here?"

"Why don't you ask them, but if you do they might wipe that grin off your face."

"What were the teachers like?" Jimmy queried.

"They were not bad, in fact they were quite good, most came out of retirement because the war was on. We had one who used to sleep at the end of the billet in his own room, he was there to make sure we never finished up fighting with one another."

"Did you ever get caught fighting?"

"Yes, but only once," continued Joe.

"What happened?"

"I had just been to the toilet before lights out, and I was coming back, when another lad twisted my arm as I passed, so I hit him, then the teacher came running out of his room and stopped us from fighting."

"What happened then?" said Jimmy.

"We both got the cane twice on each hand, but I must admit I was more embarrassed than hurt,"

"Why?" asked Jimmy.

Before Joe could answer, a smile lit up his face.

"Well I was standing in front of the teacher and this lad, and the rest of the billet were hanging out of their beds laughing, because I was standing there starkers, being caned."

"You mean you had no pyjamas on?" said the amused Jimmy.

"That's right, I didn't even own a pair of bloody pyjamas, nor did most of the other lads, so we slept in the raw. If you had none you had to sleep in your birthday suit."

"I don't think I would have liked that," said Jimmy, "but then I never got evacuated, I lived out in the country."

"When we were lying in our bunks we used to listen to 'The Man in Black' at nine o'clock every week," said Joe.

"Who was 'The Man in Black'?" asked Jimmy.

"He was an actor and he told the story, I think his name was Valentine Dyall, and it was a sort of ghost story or something like that. It was scary any way. Some of the lucky lads would be eating sweets and cake, sent from home, while the rest of us lay there watching them feeding their faces until lights went out."

The banter continued between the two new recruits.

"What happened the next morning? Did you have to see the Headmaster after fighting in the barrack room?" asked Jimmy.

"Oh no, it would be forgotten about, we would be too busy getting washed and dressed to get on to the Parade Ground."

"But why did you have to go onto the Parade Ground?" said a surprised Jimmy.

"We had to be inspected by the Headmaster and the teachers."

"Why didn't you go for breakfast first?"

"Because that's what we had to do," replied Joe. "Every morning was the same, out onto the Parade Ground, standing to attention. We would march round, then, after a while we would march over to the dining room for our breakfast. Once outside the dining room we had to stand to attention, then we would march in single file, and we would be in the same order, and go to the same chair every day for our breakfast, dinner and supper. When we all got to our chairs we would be told to stand easy, which meant we could sit down."

"You mean you had to do all that just to get your breakfast?" said Jimmy, looking in disbelief. "Sure you weren't in Borstal," he added with a smile.

"Well I have never been in such a place, so I would not know what goes on there. Perhaps you do?"

"No, I have not been in Borstal either," said Jimmy, his hand across his heart. "Did you enjoy being in 'Martin's Camp'?"

"Yes, I suppose we all did, although it was strange for evacuees to be in such a place but there was only one thing that we never liked about it," continued Joe.

"Well, what was that?" enquired Jimmy.

"It might seem strange to you, Jimmy, but the

Catholics and Protestants never mixed."

"What do you mean, they never mixed, didn't they like one another?" asked Jimmy, looking up from the chore of polishing his boots.

"Of course they did," continued Joe, "some of my mates were Protestants, but they kept us apart, the Catholics on one side of the camp and the Protestants on the other side, even on the Parade Ground and in the dining room."

"Who was responsible for that Joey-boy?" said Jimmy.

"It's Joe."

"You mean it was you?"

"No, I don't mean it was me, Jimmy. My name is not Joey-boy it's Joseph or Joe."

"OK, it's Joe but you don't mind if I call you Joey-boy?"

"Alright, I give in," protested Joe. "It must have been some officials in grey suits," Joe continued. "We even had separate barrack rooms and plots of land."

"What do you mean, you had plots of land, Joey-boy?"

"Well, when we arrived at the camp we were given a little plot of land so we could grow vegetables."

"Did you like growing vegetables?" Jimmy queried.

"Yes, it was fun, we would go into the fields down the road, and pick the cow dung up with our hands and put it into buckets so we could use it for manure on our plots."

"You mean you would put your hands into cow shit?" asked Jimmy with a look of distaste.

"It made good manure," protested Joe.

"Maybe so, but couldn't you have used some other source of manure?"

"We did, we used horse shit. We would follow the

horses when they were walking in the country lanes and when they were in the fields."

"Yes, and I suppose you still used your hands to put it in the buckets"?

"We didn't have shovels, so what else could we do, Jimmy?"

"I don't know but I suppose you would go and eat your dinner after that?"

"Yes," said a smiling Joe, "but we washed our hands first!"

"I would not have liked to have sat next to you in the classroom after you had been on one of your dung gathering exercises. You sure you went to school in 'Martin's Camp'?"

"Sure I did. I was in Daddy Rimmer's class. Not that we did much, he would tell us stories most of the time we were there."

"Were they good stories Joe?"

"Some were true stories, but I think he used to make most of them up."

"Daddy Rimmer told us that he was a Seanchai."

"What does that mean, it sounds like a Roman word?"

"It's Irish, Gaelic, for storyteller."

"Could the other teachers tell all sorts of stories?"

"I suppose they could, I can only remember Daddy Rimmer though," said Joe. "I suppose the Sergeant will tell a few tall stories before we finish with National Service and I bet he won't be as nice as Daddy Rimmer."

"He will be more concerned about being able to see his face in my boots," said Jimmy, the smile gone from his countenance. "The camp had a sort of Quarter-Master Store and I think the Headmaster had the key to it. You see I remember having holes in my shoes when I first arrived at the camp and I was taken by Daddy Rimmer to see the Headmaster, who examined my shoes, then he produced a pair of heavy boots from this little storeroom. I thought it was my birthday or something, I had never seen a pair of boots like them."

"Did you have to bull them up the way we are doing ours?" asked Jimmy, who was becoming more interested in Joe's adventure.

"Well not in the same way but we had to be clean and tidy or we would be told off. On a Saturday morning, after getting my new boots, I went into Northwich with the rest of the lads. Most of us would buy jars of peanut butter with our pocket money and also metal studs to hammer into our boots so that we could sound like real soldiers when we went on parade."

"Why did you buy peanut butter?" asked Jimmy.

"It was because we could not buy sweets from the shops, they never had any because of the war."

"Do you still like peanut butter, Joey-boy?"

"You must be joking, I hate the stuff now, I ate so much of it when I was a kid." Joe's eyebrows came closer together at the thought of the taste of peanut butter.

Jimmy laughed at the distortions on Joe's face. "Perhaps the Sergeant will let us go down the road for some and that would really make you feel at home, Joe."

"I would not eat that stuff now if you paid me."

"Are you sure you are not having me on about this 'Martin's Camp' business, I know I am a country lad, and not a Scouser like you, but I'm not daft?"

"No, I am not having you on. It was like an adventure, at least it was when I was only eleven. Not that we liked being away from home; far from it. There were times when we would think about escaping and making our own way back to Bootle and some of the older lads did manage to get away. Those in charge of the camp treated us well, but putting a couple of hundred young boys in an Army Camp was not an ideal situation. It was easier on the tougher lads, but for those who had been used to having their mams tucking them up in bed at night it must have been very hard. Maybe that's why we had 'pee the beds' in the camp. Just as well we had people like Daddy Rimmer for our teacher, he must have known how we felt."

Jimmy had forgotten about his boot polishing, his eyes were firmly fixed on Joe. "Come to think of it, Joe, I don't feel I'm too happy about being away from my girlfriend, I wish she was tucking me up tonight, instead of having to sleep in this billet, listening to this motley crew snoring."

"Never mind, Jimmy, maybe we can get the sergeant to tuck you in."

"Do you think it did you and the rest of the lads any harm?" asked Jimmy.

"No I don't think so, I suppose in many ways it will help us stand up to some of the knocks life has got in store for us," was the reply.

"You mean like facing up to this sergeant?"

"I don't think he will do me any harm, although I am not too sure about you. If you don't get those boots bulled up, he might be showing you where to find a big bag of spuds that need peeling," said Joe with a grin.

"I doubt if the sergeant would do that," smiled Jimmy.

Jimmy's manner was beginning to make an impression on Joe. Within minutes of meeting this personable young man, Joe was drawn into revealing a chapter in his young life that had, until now, been dormant. Joe's new surrounding in the Army Camp as a National Service man had triggered his thoughts, and Jimmy was the catalyst that brought forth experiences that had never been revealed to another living soul.

"The smell is the same, Jimmy."

"What smell, Joey-boy?" said Jimmy.

"In this place – it's the same."

"You mean from the 'pee the beds'?"

"No, the smell in the barrack room. Even the soap and towels are the same as those we used in 'Martin's Camp'. It's the same odour."

"What do you mean, Joey-boy, odour?"

"Never mind, carry on bulling your boots," said Joe.

"What other things did you do, Joey-boy, apart from going to school and marching around the camp like a bunch of boy scouts?"

"They would take us to an assault course, then they would say, "Right lads off you go and let's see who gets to the far side first." So away we would go like March Hares climbing up nets, swinging on ropes, running over logs across a stream, then crawling under barbed wire."

"Did they ever lose any of you?"

"Not that I know of," smiled Joe.

"When did you eat your sandwiches, Joey-boy, was it while you were impaled on the barbed wire?"

"No, I think it was when we were standing on our hands," replied Joe.

"I don't fancy running over an assault course, Joey-boy. After all I am a gentle country boy, my father is a Taxidermist," explained Jimmy, as though it was something to be proud of.

"Yes and my old man is a docker," said Joe.

"And what's a docker?" asked a puzzled Jimmy.

"Well, I'll tell you." Joe looked up from the brightness that was starting to radiate from his polished boots. "A docker is a man who works hard with no time to sit around stuffing birds and animals all day."

Jimmy chose not to comment on that.

"Do you think my boots have attained the necessary

bulling that is demanded by those in charge, Joey-boy?"

"Well if what you have said just means, do your boots have a good shine on them, you had better ask Daddy Rimmer."

"Who?"

"I mean the Sergeant," replied Joe, lifting his shining boots. "This is what the sergeant will be looking for; a pair of shining boots like this."

Joe had by now started to feel at ease, as this camp had been, after all, his home during the war, albeit under a different name!

THE WEAKER SEX?

My emotions ran high as I looked into the battered but clear photograph. A relation had just discovered it in an old chest, tucked away in the back of one of the drawers. There were about 38 women, and 10 men. I looked at the faces, many of which I recognized from my childhood, and their eyes, though frozen in time, seemed to stare back at me.

I tried hard to put a name to each of them; some came easily but others took a little more time to slot into place. Many of the names of the people who were looking out at me had receded into the depths of my mind; clouded over by the erosion of time. It was as though it was trying to hold back a lifetime of stored knowledge of those who had passed through my life. The more I searched my mind, the more the cloud was being pushed back, like the sun breaking through, and all the people I had known seemed to be willing me to remember them.

The task was a pleasant one and the names came forward slowly, one after the other. Some names came to me much easier than others, it was perhaps because they had had more of an effect on my life than others. One woman whose face caught my eyes first was Mrs. Dixie. She sat between two large ladies; a diminutive figure with a smile that gave her cheeks a pleasant roundness. Whenever I think of Mrs. Dixie, I think of her pushing her handcart every day through the streets of Liverpool selling fruit and vegetables but mostly vegetables, as fresh fruit was hard to come by in the war years of the 1940s. The photograph was taken just before Mrs. Dixie and her neighbours set out on a mystery coach trip that was to take her and her friends out into the countryside for a few hours, to relax in a country pub away from the toil of feeding and caring for their families in their closely knit community.

Mrs. Dixie was much admired and respected by her neighbours. This little lady, who set a good example to them all, was out of her bed no later than five o'clock on six mornings each week; hail, rain or snow. If you wanted to feed yourself and your kids you had to be prepared to put up with the suffering. When you are young you cannot be expected to feel or understand the pain that women like Mrs. Dixie had to contend with every day of their lives.

When she was not engaged in pushing her handcart and selling her wares, people would be knocking on her door, in the hope that she would be able to get them a clothing ticket off Mr. Levy; who was affectionately known as the Jewman. Mrs. Dixie was a collecting agent for him, and every Friday evening at six o'clock he would knock on the door, which was nearly always open for him.

"Are you there, Missus?" he would shout.

"Oh come in, Mr. Levy," she would reply, and he would walk into the living room, to find her sitting at a highly scrubbed table which smelt strongly of carbolic soap. Next to Mrs. Dixie was an empty chair, ready for Mr. Levy. On the table in front of her were small amounts of coinage stacked in little piles, one or two pound notes under the sugar basin and her little notebook, with the stub of a pencil tucked inside of it. After making himself comfortable, Mr. Levy would open his order book in front of him and the scene was set for the weekly ritual of their little business venture.

"Well what have you got for me this week, Missus?"

"Everyone has paid, except Billy McGuire," she said. "Could he pay three shillings next week, because he's had no work lately, and he's a good lad?"

"I suppose if he hasn't any money we will just have to wait until next week," said Mr. Levy.

"How right you are," agreed Mrs. Dixie. "I've collected three pounds, nineteen shillings and sixpence."

Mr. Levy checked the amount then, turning to Mrs. Dixie with a smile, pushed the commission he paid her each week towards her. "You've done well this week, Missus."

Mrs. Dixie put her little commission of 15% into her purse.

"Well now, who wants what, this week, Missus?"

"Tommy Davies could do with a new pair of boots, he's just got a job on the docks."

"Right, so he wants boots? What size?" continued Mr. Levy, who was writing on a small ticket not much bigger than a large stamp. This would be given to Tommy Davies, to take into town to exchange at a clothing warehouse for a pair of boots.

"Can I have a ticket for Mrs. Conner's eldest lad? He's getting married in two weeks' time to Mrs. Daly's youngest daughter and he needs a new suit."

While Mr. Levy was writing the details on the tickets for Mrs. Dixie's neighbours, she was pouring boiling water into the large teapot on the table next to her. This was then left to brew on the brass hob in front of the coal fire at her back.

When the business was concluded, Mrs. Dixie reached for the brown teapot and poured a cup for them both.

"Your stomach must be as tanned as the inside of this teapot. You're just as bad as that man of mine with your strong tea," said Mrs. Dixie.

"Well, you're drinking it, Missus."

"Yes, but only when I make it for you and that husband of mine," she replied.

"Anyway, this is the way it is with you women, if you

30

weren't telling me and that man of yours off, you would be having a go at the poor cat."

"Indeed I would not!" she said.

Mr. Levy smiled, and continued sipping his tea.

"Nobody touches that mug, I keep it just for you," she said.

"I know, Missus, you tell me every week that you save it just for me."

"Oh! do I?" Mrs. Dixie's cheeks flushed, and she moved uneasily on her chair.

"Anyway, its good of you to do that just for me," reassured Mr. Levy.

"While I think on, Mrs. McCarthy could do with a new pair of pants for one of her boys. She lost her husband yesterday, and the lad hasn't a decent set of clothes for his father's funeral."

Mr. Levy looked up over the top of his specs. "How sad, Missus."

"How right you are, Mr. Levy, and to think one day we will all go the same way, if God spares us."

"I wish you would have told me this before I put my ledger away, Mrs. Dixie."

Mr. Levy chose not to get involved any further on the subject and continued to make another ticket out for Mrs. McCarthy. Silence prevailed over the sparsely furnished room until a hissing sound from the gas mantle above Mr. Levy's head disturbed the peaceful scene, and the light was deflected to fall like a veil about him on to the bare table.

It was easy to picture the scene that Mrs. Dixie and Mr. Levy played out every Friday like a recurring theatrical performance. The banter from the two of them was imprinted and stored away in my mind; fond memories that had been brought out of storage by the old photograph that beckoned me to look deep within.

"Well, I'll be going, Missus," said Mr. Levy, closing his order book, before putting the loose coinage into a small black bag made of a shiny leather. "Do you mind if I go down the yard before I go Mrs?"

"Of course I don't, you should know that by now, Mr. Levy."

He turned the handle of the rim-lock and walked out into the small back yard, to be guided by the faint glow from the gaslight that shone through the kitchen window on to the yard, giving him a chance to grope his way along the wall until his hand reached out for the latch to the lavatory door.

Once inside, in total darkness, he began feeling his way for the middle of the pan, in order to aim dead centre while relieving himself. Then, after buttoning up his fly front, his hand swept across the width of the lavatory to reach the chain that hung from the high-level cistern. Returning from the yard, Mr. Levy gently closed the kitchen door, picked up his cash bag and the rest of the items used in his trade as a credit draper, and bid Mrs. Dixie good night.

"Good night, Mr. Levy, good night and God bless."

Mrs. Dixie and Mr. Levy had played out this ritual every Friday evening for many years. A lad would always be on call to run errands for the hard working Mrs. Dixie. He would sometimes deliver the clothing tickets to some of the people who had requested them. Others would be knocking on the door of the little terraced house before Mr. Levy was halfway up the street. The long wait over, they emerged from behind their house curtains as Mr. Levy went on his way. Smiles would be on the faces of the women folk; clutching their clothing tickets after leaving Mrs. Dixie's house.

This sea of faces from the photograph could tell a thousand stories. Admiration could be felt for them with their struggle to survive. They would be thankful for a trip by coach into the countryside for a few hours once or twice a year, organized by the very able Mrs. Mills; another of the smiling women on the photograph. Relaxing in the local Pub would always finish the few hours spent in the country.

The fond memories of Mrs. Dixie and the rest of them were to be imprinted on my mind forever, and to think of those stupid politicians going on about women becoming the breadwinners in this new-enlightened age. They had never been the weaker sex!

GEORGIE, AND FREDDY HORATIO MARINER

Georgie never liked school very much, but then school never liked him either. Nevertheless he was a good boy and fairly well mannered for his tender years. He did not spend much time with his mother as he lived with his grandmother in her house. Nobody knew why he never stayed at home but this was in the days when grandmothers were known to be wise. Georgie's mother lived about fifteen miles away in Bootle, whereas his grandmother lived in a place called Huyton.

Georgie knew well enough that he was hopeless at school, as did the teachers, who would make him sit at the back of the class so he would be out of the way. However, due to this, he was sometimes unable to hear all that was going on. He knew his school work was not up to the standard expected, but then most of the other lads in his class were not much better than he was, so Georgie never felt out of place. Just like most of the lads in his class he was never commended for his work. As a matter of fact, Georgie could never recall any comment other than complaints from the teachers. He never really blamed them though, because he knew that there were far too many children in the class, and the teachers were fighting a losing battle to instil anything short of the absolute basics of education into them.

The only thing that Georgie ever won at school was a bar of chocolate; a very big one, not like the ones you could buy in the local shops. Somebody had given the chocolate to his teacher; probably one of the other lads' fathers, because only someone who travelled abroad could have a bar of chocolate that size. It must have come from a foreign country, possibly America. Well anyway, Georgie won the bar of chocolate and of course all the other lads in his class wanted some, so he shared it out between them and it was generally agreed that Georgie was a great lad. This opinion lasted about as long as the chocolate.

When he got home from school that day, Georgie told his grandmother about the prize and she was pleased when he told her that he had shared it with the other boys in his class. Winning the bar of chocolate however did not stop Georgie from sagging school. He only ever sagged for half a day, never a full day. Not like Freddy Horatio Mariner, who would stay away from school whenever he could. Freddy was always getting the cane and it never seemed to bother him, at least he never showed it.

Freddy's Dad was a seaman, and the teacher said he would not make a good sailor like his father because he was always absent from school, but Freddy said he was not bothered whether he ever went to sea or not. Georgie liked Freddy Horatio Mariner because he always shared his sweets with him. Georgie's grandmother never had much money, but Freddy's father always had money when he came home from sea; not that it lasted very long, because he was always getting himself drunk, and Freddy said that his mother would then empty his Dad's pockets. When he put his pants on the next morning he would think he had spent all his money in the pub the night before. He would then ask his wife to go and borrow some from a moneylender so he could go to the pub again. Freddy's Mam would pretend to go, then she would lend him some of his own money but he never did catch on that it was his own he was borrowing.

One day, Georgie and Freddy Horatio Mariner, who lived in the same road, were on their way to school together, and Georgie told Freddy that his grandmother was baking a cake for his ninth birthday and she had said that he could bring along some of his friends to a party.

"That would be smashin'," Freddy said, "so now that it's your birthday we can stay off school."

"But that's saggin'," said Georgie.

"I know, but it is your birthday. We can go to the Pier Head and see the ships comin' in," suggested Freddy.

"Me Gran will find out and tell the teacher," said Georgie.

"No one will find out because no one goes to the Pier Head during the week. They only go at weekends," replied Freddy,

"Are ya sure?" said Georgie.

"Yeah honest," answered Freddy.

"We will have to get back home in time for my party," said Georgie.

"Don't worry, we will be home in good time," said a very confident Freddy.

So off they went to the Pier Head to see the ships, and on the way Freddy bought some sweets from Missie Murphy's shop.

"You've always got money, Freddy Horatio Mariner," said Georgie.

"Well, me Dad's a seaman isn't he," answered Freddy. Georgie just looked at Freddy and kept quiet.

"Georgie, why do you always call me Freddy Horatio Mariner?" asked Freddy.

"Well, it's your name isn't it," suggested Georgie.

"Yes, but why can't you call me Freddy like everybody else?"

"Teacher never calls you Freddy. She says, 'Freddy Horatio Mariner,' so that's what I call you," replied Georgie.

"Oh, I give up with you, Georgie," said Freddy with a look of disgust.

The two nine-year-olds soon forgot about everything else as they carried on their journey to the Pier Head.

"Do you think we will see any ships when we get

there?" asked Georgie.

"Of course we will. It's a well-known fact they're always there."

"I hope me Gran doesn't find out about me not being at school," said Georgie.

"She won't find out; and anyway I keep telling you it's your birthday isn't it, and who's goin' to tell her?" reiterated Freddy.

The two boys wandered along appearing aimless, not altogether sure if they were walking in the right direction for the Pier Head. Freddy started to chase a flock of pigeons that had landed in front of him, running into them with his arms stretched out, making a noise like an aeroplane so the birds flew off as he came charging at them.

A man suddenly stopped them and asked, "What school do you two go to?"

Freddy looked up with horror on his young face, as the man repeated the question, looking straight at Georgie.

"St Mary's," replied Georgie, with as much authority as he could muster.

"Then why aren't you at school?"

"Because its Georgie's birthday," replied Freddy.

"I see, and what is your name?"

"His name is Freddy Horatio Mariner," answered Georgie.

"Oh and I suppose your name is Admiral Nelson?" said the man.

"No, it's Georgie sir," replied the lad with a pained expression on his face.

The man looked at them both and said, "I will be reporting you both to your Headmaster."

The next day, when the boys went to school, they were told to go and report to the Headmaster.

"Come in," he shouted when the boys knocked at the door. "I believe you two boys decided to take the afternoon away from school yesterday. Is that right?"

"Well it was Georgie's birthday, sir," protested Freddy.

The Headmaster looked angry. "Oh, so is that a good enough reason for sagging school?"

The boys stood in silence.

"Right, I will deal with both of you now. Sit over there," he said, pointing to Georgie, "and next time I assure you, you will think twice about sagging school."

"But sir," Freddy protested once more, "it was Georgie's birthday."

"Well I have a little birthday present I wish to give the pair of you. First you, Freddy Horatio Mariner. Stand over by my desk."

He pushed Freddy's face down on the desk, and then the cane came crashing down across his buttocks, six times in rapid succession. Freddy was yelling blue murder as he ran out of the Headmaster's office; as if the devil himself was after him. The Headmaster then turned his attention to Georgie.

"Now, what about you my lad?"

Poor Georgie was so terrified that he wet himself. The Headmaster saw the pool getting wider on the polished floor.

"Right my lad, I see you have learned this lesson well, now clear out." The two boys went home from school, one with a sore backside, and the other with dented pride. Freddy told his Dad that it was Georgie's birthday and that's why they sagged school.

"I hope it's not another lad's birthday tomorrow ya daft sod," said his father, landing Freddy a blow. "Ya can't go sagging school every time somebody has a birthday."

Freddy gave his Dad a funny look, but kept his mouth shut in case he got another clout.

The two young friends met up on the way to school the next morning.

"I don't want to go to school, me Gran is going to tell me Uncle Barny," said Georgie.

"Well he won't kill ya will he?" protested Freddy. "I don't want to go to school either even though me Dad gave me a right clout,"

"I'll bet that hurt?" asked Georgie

"It sure did, me Dad's a big bully."

"Well that's two smacks you've had, and I've had none," said Georgie.

Freddy stayed silent unable to find the words to answer his young friend.

"I want to go home to my Mam's," moaned Georgie.

"But she lives miles away in Bootle," said Freddy.

"I know that but you can come with me," pleaded Georgie.

"You're afraid your Uncle Barny will give you a hiding tonight?"

"No, I'm not!" said Georgie.

"Anyway, I don't see why I got the cane and you didn't. That's not fair, it was your birthday after all," answered Freddy.

The two nine-year-olds continued to argue about the rights and wrongs of it; Freddy accusing Georgie of sagging, and Georgie blaming Freddy. Neither one was prepared to admit that they never wanted to go back to school.

"We could walk to the Pier Head, and, when we get there I know the way to my Mam's house," said Georgie.

"What do ya mean? I'm not going to your Mam's house. You can go on your own," said an indignant Freddy.

But after a short debate on the merits of going to Georgie's Mam's or going to school, Freddy and Georgie were soon on their way to Bootle via the Pier Head. Without a penny in their pockets the two little lads started following the direction of the trams, in the hope that they would lead them in the right direction.

"Have you got any money, Freddy Horatio Mariner?"

"No I haven't. Have you? And it's Freddy, why can't ya call me Freddy like everybody else?"

Georgie chose not to answer his young friend. Instead he pointed to the number 10 tram that was heading towards them. The double-decker, which had a horizontal advertisement for a well-known brand of whisky, seemed to float along, shaking like a large jelly. The friction of the metal wheels against the iron tram lines gave out a steady rhythm that was pleasing to the ear, as it trundled towards the Pier Head.

"We could have been on that tram if we had some money," said Freddy, pulling off his navy blue jacket to allow the faint breeze to engulf him, giving him some little comfort from the rays of the hot sun in the cloudless sky. "We've walked a long way, Georgie," he continued.

"Yeah we have," replied Georgie. "Do ya wanna sit down for a bit?"

Freddy nodded in agreement. The boys sat with their backs against the front of a baker's shop, and Freddy pushed his navy blue jacket underneath him to ease the soreness that he was still feeling from the caning that had been given to him by his Headmaster the day before. Georgie's head turned towards the door of the shop, the smell of freshly baked bread and cakes giving his tummy a funny feeling.

"How much further is it to the Pier Head?" Freddy asked Georgie, while pulling the remaining sweets from the lining of his pocket.

"I don't think it's too far," said Georgie, stuffing his sweet, which looked remarkably like a little hairy creature, into his mouth.

"Are ya sure it's not a long way?" insisted Freddy.

"Well I don't think it is," said Georgie on the defensive. "Me Mam makes scouse, and she will give you some when we get to our house."

"What's that?" asked Freddy, a puzzled expression on his young face.

"It's meat and potatoes and other things," replied Georgie.

He accepted Georgie's explanation of what scouse was and they set off again on the long walk to Bootle. Freddy was dragging his jacket along the ground and told Georgie that his legs were tired and that they must have walked miles. Georgie never answered but he too had discarded his jacket and allowed it to trail along the pavement. The bright, clear blue sky started to give way to dark gathering clouds as the afternoon moved on and the large buildings of the Pier Head came into sight. A cool breeze gathered pace and the temperature started to drop, and, as they looked up, the time on the face of the Liver Building clock did not register as they walked in silence. The wind and rain came from the river and drove into them as they quickly struggled into their jackets making them like wet blankets. The wind gave them no quarter as it dragged their little bodies from side to side as they struggled to stay upright, in order to reach the open space in front of the Liver Building.

"Over there, look Freddy Horatio Mariner, there it is, it's the number 10 tram. If we watch the way it goes out, we can follow the lines to Bootle," said Georgie on reaching the safety of the tram shelter.

"You're daft, Georgie, there's tramlines running everywhere."

"Honest, Freddy when we see the tram go out I'll know the way, because this is the way me Gran takes me to my Mam's." The two rain-soaked and dejected boys now set off on the second leg of their journey, their feet squelching in sodden shoes and woollen socks which had gathered around their ankles in a crumpled mass, adding to the misery that had overtaken them. Georgie's eyes kept searching through the blinding rain for some sort of landmark and at last he recognized a church on the far side of the road, which he always looked out for as a landmark when he was on the tram with his gran.

The church had no railings or grounds, and its stone front came out onto the pavement. At that moment the voice of a woman called out to the boys from the gothic shaped doorway. They ran across the road to her and into the shelter of the doorway. She looked at the pitiful sight before her and asked them why they were not at school. Freddy froze, as he could see the sight of the Headmaster's cane towering above his head.

"We've been to the Pier Head to see the ships," replied Freddy, hoping his explanation would do the trick. The woman smiled at the two boys and gave them each a sweet.

"What's your name?" she asked.

"Mine is Georgie, and this is Freddy Horatio Mariner."

"Freddy who? Oh I see. Freddy. That's a nice name. Where are you going?"

"To me Mam's in Bootle."

"Now you wait here and I will put you on the tram when it comes," continued the woman. She put the two boys on the first tram that came along, paid their fare and told the conductor where to put them off. When they arrived at their destination, the boys walked along the street towards Georgie's house with the rain still beating down on their heads.

Georgie pushed open the unlocked front door and walked in to the smell of cooking sausages. In the grate was a roaring fire, and its warm glow engulfed them. Georgie's mother walked into the living room when she heard the boys enter.

"Oh my God, where did you two come from? You look

like drowned rats. Who's that?" her eyes fixing on Freddy.

"It's Freddy Horatio Mariner, he goes to school with me," replied her son.

"It doesn't look like he's been to school with you today. You had better sit down and we'll sort things out later."

Freddy smiled at Georgie when he saw the two plates of sausages.

"Eat them up, then we'll decide what we will do with the pair of ya."

After eating their fill, they collapsed from exhaustion while Georgie's mum got a message to Freddy's home as to where he was for the night. Early the next morning she took them back to Huyton. Freddy's mum then escorted them to school where they were punished again by the Headmaster.

THE ROOM

A small sized room, a small sized bed, four
Young boys lay head to toe, all sleeping and
Breathing in perfect harmony, a foot
Projecting out of a well worn blanket, the
Twitching of a toe taps against a brotherly
Nose in slumber dreams.

All dreaming, not two the same, one gliding
Into the sky holding the string of a kite, the
One beside him dreams of a big bed with lots
Of nice clean sheets and only his head to rest
On a nice soft pillow.

At the bottom of the bed, one is dreaming of
Sitting on a fast moving train, the whistle
Blowing the steam engine towing, the last of
The dreamers is dreaming of school, a teacher
Sits at the head of the class, a voice in the
Distance a faint sound in his ears.

No wardrobe against the wall or covering on
The floor, no curtains to cover a naked
Window, just dust and grime from out-
Pouring chimney stacks, the ceiling all
Cracked and bare, looks down on many bare
Feet that twitch when a fly descends.

Four young heads a sleep on a bed without a
Pillow, gentle soft breathing like a soft breeze
In spring, the walls once papered with bright
Coloured flowering design, hang faded with
Turned up edges, meet skirting boards that
Once knew paint.

A door without a catch, painted many times, not
Smooth but rough to touch, hangs creaking when
Pushed against the foot of the bed, a floor of
Wood scrubbed white with smelly liquid soap
Makes nostrils twitch when newly scrubbed and
Flies and lice hurry to hide away.

Four pair of short pants lay on the floor in
Disarray and not a sign of under pants, for
Who can shed what has never been worn, and
On a shelf. A masterly draughtsman's drawing
Of an merchant ship, displaying the colours of
The shipping master in circles round the stack.

A weary mother stands at the bottom of the
Bed and looks down into the faces of her
Offsprings, her face and thoughts project love
And hope for her young sons. A reassuring
Voice penetrates their ears as she calls out to
Them, their bright eyes catch hers and love
Fills the air.

ADDICOT'S PAWNSHOP

Jamie Campbell was about five foot five with coal black hair, and very bushy eyebrows. His big bright blue eyes would hold you in their gaze when you looked into his face and the sides of his mouth would turn up as a smile spread from ear to ear. He was slightly built, yet his arms were covered in black hair. Nature was wasting no time in turning him into a young man, which was just as well because he had entered the stage in his early life when he would have to work for a living. The cosy fireside and the Christmas tree adorned with presents and the counting of Easter eggs at the festive season were never part of Jamie's young life, but his parents had given him whatever they could afford to keep him healthy and strong.

The walk from his house seemed to go on forever as he thought about what lay ahead for him. Jamie was turning over in his mind what the man had said to him at the job interview.

"You must be clean and tidy and get here early each morning. We start work at eight o'clock on the dot, so you must make sure you arrive here on time."

Jamie could see it was only twenty-to-eight by the clock fixed to the back wall of the pawnshop in the street, its big round face looking out onto the main road inviting people to stare in through the shop window. His mother had made sure her son was well turned out to start his first job. He wore an open-neck check shirt with short sleeves and a navy blue V-neck pullover with no sleeves. The jacket that he used to wear for school was folded over his right arm because the sun was shining and it was too hot to wear it.

Jamie's grey pants were a bit shoddy and the creases had disappeared but they were clean. His shoes had a dullness about them because Jamie had used spit on the shoe brush because there was no black polish in the house. Jamie looked at the big old house that had been turned into a pie factory. The man at his interview told him that they made meat pies as well as other foodstuffs. He was feeling a little nervous, walking towards the side entrance door, when he felt a heavy hand rest on his shoulder.

"Come on lad or you will be late for work."

Jamie looked up towards the voice, and a tall man with a big beaked nose looked down at him and ushered him through the doorway and into the pie factory.

As the rest of the workforce came into the building, some of them greeted him while others just looked and ignored him. Jamie had never seen so much food in his life, and at lunchtime he was given something to eat by the lady who made the pies, so he did not have to eat the brawn sandwiches, covered in brown sauce, that his mother had prepared for him. Jamie's first day earning a living seemed to go on forever, there was no big clock to look at like the one in Addicot's pawnshop but the day went well for him. He felt comfortable, in a nervous sort of way, working with the people who were showing him his duties, but he yearned for the working day to come to an end. Then he could rush home to tell his Mam what his first day was like, seeing all those meat pies and ham shanks being cooked.

At last it was going home time, so he climbed the steps from the basement, leaving the cooked ham shanks and meat pies made that day, ready for the van in the morning. While Jamie stood with the others waiting to put his card into the time clock machine he noticed the man with the big beaked nose, standing in line with the rest of the workforce, waiting for the clock to strike five. He had no jacket on and his shirtsleeves were turned up as he kept flexing the muscles in his forearms. Most people took no notice of him, but Jamie smiled as he thought the beaked nose man looked a lot like Popeye.

The next morning the sun was still shining as Jamie made his way to work feeling not quite so nervous about the pie factory. He looked into Addicot's window and the clock was showing twenty-to-eight but it would be more than an hour before the shop was open for business. Jamie had grown up seeing the sight of women going to the pawnshop in the morning when he was on the way to school.

Monday was the main day for parting with their possessions as what little house-keeping money they had would be spent by then. Some of the women were old and had bundles of bedding balanced on their heads, and others were younger standing there with their children. Some would be trying to hold on to the kids with one hand while balancing the bundle on their heads with the other. His young mind never wondered what would be on their beds for the rest of the week, but he did know what happened when his mother went to the pawnshop on a Monday morning with his Dad's new shoes. He would have to wear his working boots all week, but he never minded them being in Addicot's just so long as the neighbours never knew they had been taken there.

Sometimes Jamie's mother would forget to redeem the pledge on Saturday morning, which always resulted in his Dad howling the house down. How could he go into the lounge bar on a Saturday night and parade about? He would have to confine himself to the common bar instead. Jamie moved on before he got too engrossed in the dealings that went on in Addicot's pawnshop. The entrance to the pie factory was in sight when Jamie spotted Beak-nose rushing to get in front of two women so he could reach the doorway of the factory first to put his card in the time clock before them.

Most of Jamie's working day was spent cleaning and

tidying up but he was getting to know more each day about the cooking of meat pies and boiled ham. The smell would make him feel hungry, and if the cook was in a good mood she would give him a hot pie for his dinner. The work was pleasant but Jamie never intended to stay forever working in the basement of the big old house making meat pies. He wanted to be able to see and mix with people during the working day instead of being stuck in a pie factory, where the only people he would see would be the cook, a few others and Beak-nose when he came down to collect the pies and ham and other goodies to put in the van for delivery.

One of the things that broke up the monotony of the day was the appearance of the two bull terriers who made their way into the basement from the offices on the top floor. The dogs would come down without the knowledge of their master who was one of the bosses. They were two friendly dogs, but Jamie thought they were slow and cumbersome. He always liked giving them titbits to eat, much against the cook's instructions as she had warned him he would be in trouble for encouraging the dogs; he could even get the sack for feeding them. The bosses were always telling people off for that, but Jamie never paid much heed to what the cook was trying to tell him, and thought there was nothing wrong with wanting to give the dogs bits of food.

Jamie himself would have loved to have a dog, but there was no room in his little terraced home with his Mam and Dad, his two brothers and his sister. The Mullens next door to Jamie had a big dog but it had to sleep in the back yard in a wooden box with a tarpaulin sheet over it. Jamie had hoped that his mother would let him build a dog kennel in the back yard but she always said, "I've already got a howling dog in the house with your father. The whole neighbourhood can hear him when I fail to collect his shoes from Addicot's on a Saturday morning."

Different members of staff would take the two dogs for a walk each day when they had finished their duties. Most days it would be Beak-nose who, after completing his deliveries with the van, would rush in to take them out. Jamie hoped that one day he would be asked to take the dogs for a walk in the park at the top of the road, and, in time his hopes were fulfilled. One day he had finished cleaning the floors in the cellar, and the tables were spotless ready for the pie making the next morning, when in walked Beak-nose, who asked the cook if Jamie could go with him to walk the two dogs. It was like music to his ears when she agreed and he lost no time in getting his coat.

The warm air and the rays of the sun greeted them as they emerged from the cool cellar at three o'clock on a beautiful mid-August day as it had been an exceptionally warm summer. The two dogs seemed pleased to be going for a walk and sat, patiently waiting, but obviously eager to be on the move. As soon as Beak-nose fastened the leads on the collars of the bull terriers, they were jumping around as dogs do when they feel happy, their short legs stamping the warm tarmac on the driveway.

"Here, you take the bitch," said Beak-nose to Jamie, "and don't go walking too fast, this sort of dog can't breath very well."

"Why not?" asked Jamie.

"I'm not sure, it's something to do with their noses being flat," he replied.

"Oh, I know what you mean. There's a fella in our street who's got a flat nose because he is always fightin' and sniffin', just like them dogs with their pudgy noses," continued Jamie.

"That's enough talk," said Beak-nose, "let's be getting on with it."

Jamie looked at his companion who was walking a

couple of paces in front of him, and he felt a sense of guilt come over him because he saw the man not as a nice person, and somehow the name of Beak-nose had become implanted in Jamie's mind. Yet this was the same man who asked that Jamie be allowed to walk the dogs with him. Jamie was sure that they were going to the park at the top of the road, but Beak-nose seemed to have other plans as they walked along the busy main road.

The two dogs kept a steady slow pace but their short legs kept putting the brakes on, so a more leisurely gait was the order of the day. Beak-nose, who was yards ahead, walked past the park entrance, with Jamie following, but on passing, the two dogs gave a sideways glance at the entrance, their pace slowing and the lead dog found his neck being pulled forward as Beak-nose gave a slight pull on the lead to let it know he was not going into the park that day. The sun was full in a cloudless blue sky and was moving towards them on its journey beyond the Wirral Peninsula, and the heat of the day did not appear to be cooling as there was no breeze. Jamie and the two dogs had no say in the route Beak-nose was taking.

He felt that they were going in the wrong direction, but would not dare ask to where they were going with the two dogs. Taking them for a walk with Beak-nose was one thing, but the fourteen year old Jamie felt he had nothing in common with this man to be able to strike up any kind of conversation, so like the two dogs he was being led by the collar to wherever it was that Beak-nose was headed for.

Jamie could feel the warmth of the pavement through the thin soles of his shoes, and wondered how the dogs must feel, with their paws closer still. He could hear the heavy stifled breathing through their podgy noses and he felt sorry for them. He could also see that Beak-nose was not at all concerned with the welfare of the dogs when their pace slackened as the walk continued in the hot sun. They eventually came to a halt as Beak-nose stopped to talk to a man who stepped out of a shop doorway. They kept a discreet distance. The two dogs were lying on their stomachs, their front paws pushed forward and their breathing still heavy. The older of the two dogs seemed to be gasping for breath.

The two men seemed to be in some sort of serious discussion and paid no attention to Jamie and the animals. Eventually Beak-nose turned to him with his hand stretched out, and pressed the lead of the other dog into his hand. The dog looked up at Beak-nose as the lead was exchanged.

"Take them back to the factory, I won't be going back, I have some business to attend to. You will be alright, just take your time," said Beak-nose.

He then turned and walked away with the other man, leaving Jamie on his own in charge of the two dogs. Jamie gently pulled the two leads and the dogs slowly, if somewhat reluctantly, got to their feet.

The older of the two animals was having more difficulty walking, and the further they went the slower was the pace of the two animals. Fear had started to grip Jamie and he felt he would never reach the factory before it closed for the day. He clung to the hope that somebody would come looking for him and the two dogs, but this did not happen. The senior of the two dogs could go no further, his breathing was so bad that he collapsed in the doorway of the Salvation Citadel. Jamie could see that it was going to be impossible to get the dog to its feet, as the female edged forward and pushed her nose, into her fallen companion's face, but there was no response.

The long walk and the heat of the day had taken its toll, and the heavy breathing ceased. Jamie panicked and tried to get help from people passing by, but his pleas went unaided. People pretended not to notice his anguish, but at last a lad, who was younger than Jamie, agreed to stand guard over the dog while Jamie made his way back to the factory with the bitch. At last he arrived back with the surviving dog in a very weak condition. Jamie was praying to himself that the dog would live, but he knew that he was in trouble because of Beak-nose. She was carried upstairs to the office by one of the men in the factory.

The boss almost fainted when he saw the state of his prize dog, and the women in the office were all crying and giving Jamie dirty looks, as though it was his fault. Then the questioning started. Eventually a member of staff was sent out in the van to bring the other dog back. The young lad who stayed on guard was rewarded with a couple of pork pies, but the dog was found to be dead. Jamie was told to go home as he would be dealt with in the morning. He had little sympathy from his parents, which was followed by a sleepless night. The next day the big clock in Addicot's pawnshop had just chimed seven-thirty as Jamie stood looking into the window hoping that it would swallow him up. His young mind was confused and he kept staring up, afraid of going to work at the pie factory, and at the same time not wanting to be late. The clock showed seven-forty-five, and Jamie made his way in with a heavy heart. It was no longer a joy to walk through the door and smell the freshly cooked meats, as he felt only fear, and was afraid of what was to meet him when he went in.

Jamie knew he had done no harm to the dogs. Beak-nose had left him to care for them on his own, but if the bosses knew the truth about what really happened, he wondered if they would realise that he was also the victim. Jamie was not sure, and he wanted to turn around and run back home. At last he was at his place of work and was sure everybody was talking about him. "You have got yourself in a right mess," said the cook.

"Yes but I …"

"Never mind telling me, it's the bosses you will have to explain to," continued the cook.

"I told them what happened last night. It was not my fault that dog died. Beak-nose, I mean the van driver, told me to bring them back on my own," protested Jamie.

"Yes but you have more explaining about the dogs when the boss questions you."

"What do you mean, Cook?" asked Jamie, puzzled by the remark.

"Never mind, I'm saying no more."

He felt very much on his own. The cook was a kind woman, but she had Jamie very worried by her remarks, and the rest of the workforce were no better. They just ignored him, making his anguish much harder to bear, every time they passed him. Beak-nose kept his distance, loading the van with goods for delivery. When he had finished he was still hanging around the yard when he should have been out delivering and Jamie felt he looked like a worried man. At last the waiting was over as a member of staff was sent to take Jamie up to the office. On his way he could see Beak-nose making his way up the stairs ahead of him. He must have heard Jamie behind him but he never looked back, not even when he reached the manager's office. Beak-nose knocked on the door and went in, just as Jamie got to the top step and was told to wait until he was called into the office, and he could hear loud voices coming from inside.

Little Jamie's nerves sent him into a state of panic, but at last the long waiting was over. Beak-nose came running out of the office slamming the door behind him and made for the stairway without so much as a glance at Jamie. He ran down the stairs, like a wild goat in flight. A woman came out and invited Jamie in. Standing behind the desk was the boss who towered above Jamie and by the window were two women with tears running down their cheeks. They had coloured handkerchiefs with which they patted their faces but they could not hold back the tide that flowed from their eyes. He heard a sob as they made eye contact with the bewildered Jamie.

"Do you realise that the two dogs have died? Have you been mating them, is that the reason you took them yesterday? So tell me lad, have you been mating them?"

"I don't know what ya mean sir by mating them?"

"Did they have sex with other dogs?"

"No sir, all we did was walk them."

The starkness of the reply from the boss brought about a flutter of the handkerchiefs and more sobs from the ladies.

"We will get to the truth of the matter because we are going to have an autopsy on them and if the findings are not in your favour I will call the police in, do you understand?"

"Yes sir," replied Jamie, not understanding most of what the boss had been saying to him.

"You and the van driver were the last two people to be seen with the two dogs, so I have no option but to dismiss you. The wages due to you can be collected when you finish work today."

Jamie could not believe what he had just heard. He looked in the direction of the sniffing ladies but they turned their backs on him to peer out of the window. He felt humiliated having to work the rest of the day with people who only knew half of what had happened to the dogs, and Beak-nose was nowhere to be seen. He was the only person who could confirm that Jamie was innocent of any wrongdoing but had stormed out of the building after his dismissal.

By the end of his last working day most people had

ceased to comment on the misfortune of the dogs and his dismissal. When Jamie went from the pie factory for the last time, the bright sunny day had given way to dark clouds and blustery rain, making his plight that much harder to bear. By the time he reached Addicot's pawnshop, the fourteen year old had already put the cruel events of the last few days behind him. Jamie only glanced in the window as he passed and he wondered whether his mother would be able to afford to get his Dad's new shoes out of pawn at the weekend now that less money would be coming into the house, as he was unable to make a contribution to the domestic purse.

Jamie's father was sitting in front of the fire when he walked in and his mother was in the kitchen and the smell of boiling cabbage permeated the small living room.

"How did you get on today?" his mother asked him from the tiny kitchen.

"I got the sack."

"Oh my God," his mother cried.

"The two dogs are dead."

"Well you never killed the bloody dogs did ya, so why did they sack you?" asked his Dad.

"Was it that bloody van driver who caused it?" his mother asked as she walked from the kitchen into the living room, wiping her hands on her apron and looking at Jamie's father sitting by the fireside with the evening paper draped across his lap. "It's terrible," she said.

"I'm going around to see them over this," said his Dad, as he lifted one of his boots from the side of the chair.

"Just you stay where you are, things are bad enough for the lad without you making things worse," she shouted at him.

"Well the dogs could not have been very healthy if they snuffed it just because the sun was shining," he protested, placing the boot back at the side of the chair.

Jamie sat down and waited for his mother to bring him a plate of potatoes and green cabbage. She always told him that it was the green cabbage that would put 'lead in his pencil'. His mind was already filled with his future plans, and he hoped he would find work very soon.

Jamie, being the likeable lad that he was, did not have to wait very long for another job to come his way. The man who owned Addicot's pawnshop had observed Jamie looking in the window on his way to the pie factory, and many a time had seen him with his mother in the shop, waiting to pawn anything that would bring in a few shillings until the weekend. Jamie jumped at the offer of working in the shop and enjoyed his new job. He didn't mind too much, swapping the smell of the pork pies and cooked ham shanks for that of bundles of bedding and sweaty shoes that he had to stow away in the back room of the pawnshop, and his strong arms had no difficulty lifting the heavy bundles onto the shelves.

At last Jamie was meeting people while learning his new trade of pawnbroker. The weeks went by and autumn had given way to winter when he had the chance to attend to the customers at the counter. The painful memory of the dirty trick that Beak-nose played on him by not telling the truth had faded into the recesses of his young mind. Jamie felt quite smug as he looked out of the shop window. The big clock on the wall ticking away at the back of him seemed so much louder because the shop was empty of customers and the only sounds came from the pages of the owner's heavy ledgers being turned over as he did his bookkeeping during a quiet spell.

Jamie could see that the street outside was empty because of the cold biting wind and he was so pre-occupied, he failed to see a customer walking into the shop.

"Jamie, serve the man," came the stern voice of his

employer. Jamie looked up to see a gent's suit draped over the high counter and a pair of new shoes being placed on the top of the suit.

"How much can I have for those?"

Jamie looked up to the sound of the familiar voice, only to find himself staring into the eyes of Beak-nose.

"I'll give you five shillings, take it or leave it," said Jamie, without waiting for his employer's assessment.

Jamie stood and watched closely as Beak-nose started to protest at the small amount offered but Jamie repeated what he had said. The man growled. "All right, if that's the best you can do, I'll take it."

"We'll make a pawnbroker of you yet," said Jamie's boss. "Go and put the kettle on, there's a good lad."

Jamie glanced out of the window in time to see Beak-nose crossing the road, pulling the collar of his jacket around his ears and clutching his meagre five shillings.

THE MAN IN THE GABARDINE OVERCOAT

It is sad the way we make snap judgements on people purely on their physical appearance. A well-dressed man or woman can often command respect, whether or not he or she is good, bad or indifferent, and a pair of shiny boots will always win the day.

I remember joining a queue of people in a café in the centre of Liverpool, waiting for my tea and toast. In front of me was a middle-aged man and when I saw his shabby and dirty appearance I instinctively stood back so that I would not be in the firing line if he had fleas, in case they wanted to change partners.

He was wearing a greyish gabardine overcoat, its true colour having long since faded due to exposure to rain and sunlight over many years. The structure of his shoes had collapsed leaving the heel of the left lying flat, causing him to shuffle his foot along whilst walking. After he had been served, I watched him make his way to the far side of the café, and by the time I sat down with my own refreshment I had put him out of my mind.

The following day I went into the café for my lunch, which is convenient because I was engaged on a job across the road, and, standing in front of me was the same man with the shabby overcoat. He seemed a little cleaner and tidier, his grey hair had a shiny gloss to it and his skin had a healthy look, even though I could only see the side of his face. However, his coat and shoes still had the look of despair about them.

Trying hard to hold my tray steady, my eyes travelled around the café looking for a place to sit. When at last I found a space at a table, its only occupant was the man with the gabardine overcoat.

"Do you mind if I sit here?" I enquired.

"Certainly, if you want to, nobody ever sits by me. You must have a pretty low opinion of yourself wanting to sit next to someone like me," came his answer.

As I sat down I tried not to smile at his comments, as I did not want to show disrespect. He was surprisingly articulate, his words seemed to flow easily and were crystal clear. His voice had a familiar tone about it, and as I looked into his face, his eyes had a glint that held my gaze.

"How are you doing lad, you don't remember me do you?"

I looked at him across my fish and chips.

"Oh yes I do, you're Davy Mortimer," I said, surprising even myself at such quick response. "Are you not having anything to eat?" I continued, my voice having a slight tremor through not wanting to offend Davy.

"No, it's alright I have money, I'm not hungry," he replied, giving me a smile that was obviously meant to reassure me. There was so much that I wanted to ask him, but I was finding a great deal of difficulty in choosing my words.

Davy seemed to understand my inner thoughts and kept on talking about days that had gone by. I was content to listen to him, but most of the time, my mind was wandering off, and the man sitting facing me was no longer the fit and able young man that I remembered when I was only a youngster. I don't know why I remembered Davy as quickly as I did when I looked into his face; maybe I was looking into his soul! This was still intact and shone like a beacon to let me see through the well worn face in front of me, to expose the fine and brave young man who had been a local hero in the days of my childhood.

He seemed to be carried away as he talked about the past. His clear voice and perfect diction was heard by the other diners, and their heads swivelled in his direction. The more he talked about the past the more I recalled mental pictures of Davy on the banks of the Liverpool Canal. He was not a big man but had inner strength. The sight of this man climbing out of the canal as the light faded on a cold January afternoon came into my mind. He was being helped by one of the three policemen who stood by as a frantic search went on, for some hours, for a child of four who had disappeared into the black waters.

He had been in the water for some time helping with the search, and was handed a blanket by one of the policemen to cover his naked body. Davy would discard his clothes without a word to anybody, then dive into the water as naked as the day he was born. He stood on the pathway only long enough to get his breath back before diving back into the freezing waters once again. Whenever the alarm went up that a child had fallen into the canal, he would be one of the first people on the scene to help the police frogmen.

Sometimes only the dead body would be recovered. However, he saved many a youngster who could go on to tell their children, and perhaps grandchildren, about the man who rescued them. I never knew if he ever received a medal or certificate for the many acts of bravery he performed but he certainly deserved one!

Apart from my brief encounter with him when I was at school with his younger brother, I knew very little about him personally, other than about his exploits in trying to save children from the canal. As the banter continued between us at the table it was clear that he knew more about me than I knew about him, and sitting by Davy had unlocked the gates of our memories. The more he talked, the more other diners turned their heads in his direction. He had a pleasant-sounding, captivating voice. Its delivery and pitch held one in its power.

The interest of the other diners, the younger ones in particular, drew them in the days to follow, to sit alongside Davy during their lunch break. Sometimes as many as nine or ten people would be seen sitting with him, listening to the wonderful tales he told about his torturous journey through life. He talked about his childhood, and he made his misfortunes seem trivial.

"I suppose you think I'm hard done by don't you? Well I might be old and grey and what you would call down on my luck but in truth I'm as free as a bird. I don't live in a cage like a lot of people who only imagine they are free. Many people burden themselves with all sorts of worries, then go on to say life is hard, but life is what you choose to make it. Sometimes we refuse to believe it when things go wrong, it's always somebody else's fault, rarely ever our own. Most of you will have had at least a cup of tea and a round of toast no matter how much down on your luck you were before you left home this morning."

Davy's young audience listened without interruption, but then a young lady interrupted his flow.

"You tell a fine tale," she said.

"Tale it might be, but just think about it," continued Davy. "Supposing you lived like most animals in the wild, every day when you awoke you would not have any idea where your next meal was coming from, or even if there was to be a next meal. If you were an animal in the wild you could not go and put the kettle on or get your parents to make you a piece of toast; you would have to go looking for food the minute you opened your eyes. Worse still for you, are you yourself to be the next meal for some other animal?

That takes place every day – to be eaten by some

other animal looking for their breakfast, or worse still it could be you who is killed by the major predator, the human animal who likes to kill just for pleasure or glory. Then after spending time in the pursuit of food you return home with enough for your young ones who are waiting for your return, because they are hungry, only you find that some other animal has eaten them."

"That tale is a bit depressing, Davy," replied another one of his young audience.

"Ah! But that's how life is for most creatures on this earth, so you should stop for a while and think how lucky you are, that you are not somebody's next meal."

For many weeks I sat, listened and watched Davy entertain his young audience. He was sharp and had an answer for every one of them, with their continual questioning of his lifestyle. Although they could not hope to fully understand his way of life, they were curious as to why he should be this way. Davy was refreshing to the young people who emerged from stuffy office blocks each day. His world was a way of life that they did not know or understand and, until now, perhaps did not want to, but seeing and listening to him every day made them assess their own values and question them. While he enjoyed the company of the young people each day, he also did not wish for any part of their lives. He seemed to be like a lonely white cloud floating by.

His eyes drew you to him like magnets that were warm and friendly. The weeks passed and I, like the rest of the diners who had become acquainted with him, always looked forward to meeting him each day. Coming into the cafeteria one day I noticed that Davy was not present, and no word was being exchanged.

When I sat down one of Davy's admirers pushed a local newspaper in front of me.

"Elderly man found dead in shop doorway covered

by a greyish gabardine overcoat."

His young friends missed him dreadfully, but none of them could possibly know just how much I did too. I could hardly contain my grief, as I was one of the children he had saved all those years before from the canal. I owed my life to Davy.

CURLY MURPHY

Curly Murphy had always kept chickens in his back yard for as long as anyone could remember. No one seemed to mind when the cock crowed in the early hours of the morning, because most people had to be up early to go to work on the docks. The chickens had the run of the small back yard, but at times this could be a nuisance. They would often get under Curly's feet whenever he wanted to go to the lavatory, which was at the bottom of the yard.

However, the crowing cock would never win any popularity contest on a Sunday morning, when neighbours expected to have an extra hour in bed before getting up to face the day. Sunday was also the one day in the week when most people in the community had time to sit down to a breakfast of saltfish. The fish was flat, and as stiff as a board when bought from the fishmonger. It would be cut up the night before and put into a big pan and left to soak overnight. Fresh water would be put in the pan and it would be left simmering on a low light on the gas stove before they went to early morning worship. By the time they got back from Church, the house would reek with the smell of the fish, and the taste buds would be brought to a peak with anticipation for their breakfast.

Curly was a tall man with big hands and flat feet and a pale complexion due to his not seeing much sunlight as he worked in a warehouse on the docks. So his hobby was a good way to inhale some fresh air into his lungs and make a few shillings from selling eggs to his neighbours to augment his meagre wages. He knew those people who lived close by would never risk upsetting him about his cock crowing on a Sunday morning, otherwise they could be deprived of cheap eggs.

He was a gentle sort of man and his only adversaries were the cats who stalked his back yard walls, but he was well able to keep them at bay with the help of the little Scots terrier, a stray who had been given to him by the foreman of his warehouse. The foreman's wife was not too keen on dogs, and he knew that by giving it to Curly it would have a good home, and he would no doubt show his appreciation in return by handing over some of the fresh eggs.

Curly, being the gentleman that he was, never looked forward to the build-up towards Christmas, because that was the time he had to think about fattening up some of his older birds for the roasting dish, if he was to please his neighbours, and culling the chickens for the festive season always created a great problem.

He could never carry out the 'coup de grace' himself to his little feathered friends and this particular Christmas, Curly was having great difficulty in finding someone to do this unwanted chore. However he was not to be beaten. He had in mind two young lads, who lived only a few doors away. So off he went to ask the boy's father if his two sons could play the part of executioner. Kevin was the older of the two by twelve months, a big lad for a fourteen year old, with broad shoulders. Brian was the quieter of the two, but he was as tall as Kevin, and it was plain to see they were going to be two fine men in the years to come.

"Sure they will help you out," said the boys' father without consulting the young lads.

"I'll give them ten shillings between them if they kill, I mean, ring the necks of ten of my hens," said Curly, the words almost choking him as they left his lips.

By this time the làds joined their father at the front door and were looking at Curly in disbelief.

"Have never killed chickens," stammered Kevin.

"Go on lads, have a go."

Their father tried to prompt them, bu̇
answered.

"How would you like to kill them foɪ
Curly, looking at the boys' father,

"Well' er' no, I would sooner leave it to the
be a bit of pocket money for them."

The lads looked at their father with a look of
submission on their young faces.

"OK, we'll do it," said Kevin, looking at Brian to see
if he agreed.

The boys knew that Curly himself did not want to do
the dirty deed. Curly led the boys to the chosen place of
execution in the basement of his house. The chickens
chosen to fill the roasting tins for the festive season had
already been selected, and were pecking away on the
basement floor having their last supper.

"Do you know what to do?" Curly asked the boys, but
they gave no answer. Brian stood with his back to the white-
washed wall, his lips sealed as he looked up at Curly.

"I don't know what to do," said the more daring Kevin.

"It's easy," said Curly.

"You're scared," came a sharp reply from Brian.

"No I'm not. It's just that I don't like killing my own
chickens," said Curly.

"Shut up, Brian and seeing that you have a lot to say,
you can kill the first five, and I will kill the rest of them,"
said Kevin.

"No, you be the first, you're older than me," retorted
Brian, his back pushed closer to the wall. Then he let out a
sharp yelp like a pup as one of the chickens brushed against
his legs.

"All right, I will do the first five, but I still don't know
what to do," cried Kevin.

"Oh, it's easy," said Curly, "you sit on that chair, then

one of the chickens and put it between your knees."

Kevin looked up at the man. The fear of the unknown started to grip him as he made his way to the chair reluctantly and sat down.

"You will have to get hold of one of the chickens first, as I have told you, they won't come to you, then press your knees tight to hold it."

"Then, why don't you do it if you know how, Curly?" asked Brian, with a grin on his face.

Curly chose not to answer. Kevin leapt onto the floor grabbing one of the birds by the leg, the rest of them scattered in fear of their lives, whilst Kevin pulled the screeching chicken back to the chair. The remaining birds gathered in the far corner, and Brian still kept close to the wall, a look of fear covering his countenance, and satisfaction spread over the face of Curly, knowing that the task was about to be carried out. Kevin sat with the chicken between his knees awaiting further instructions.

"Pull its wings down by its side then press your knees tight against its side and put your two hands around its neck, and twist. It's easy," said Curly.

"You keep telling us its easy, then why don't you do it, instead of getting our kid to do it," said Brian, his back still holding the wall up.

Kevin looked towards Brian as he tightened his grip around the neck of the chicken, and Brian put his hands to his face shielding his eyes from the scene unfolding before him.

A silence descended on the basement, and, strange as it seemed, the rest of the hens were not the slightest bit bothered by what was going on and continued to peck away at scraps on the floor. Kevin twisted the neck of the chicken like twisting the top off a bottle. The head came away in Kevin's strong hands and he dropped it onto floor and as he loosened his grip on the headless bird it ran around the basement then slumped at the feet of the terrified Curly who tried not to show his fear.

The booming voice of the boys' father broke the silence. "How are my courageous young fellas getting on?" His fat frame leant against the door.

The boys did not answer and Curly just gave a nod. The boys' father looked at the headless chicken then started to give Kevin advice on how to do the job properly.

"Would you like to show Kevin how it's done, Dad?" said Brian, recovering from his ordeal.

"Well 'er no like, I think Kevin's got the hang of it without me showing him."

"What you mean Dad, you and Curly are too scared to do it yourselves?" continued Brian.

"No, it's not like that, I'm thinking of you and Kevin getting the ten shillings. Isn't that right, Curly?"

A nod of the head was the only gesture Curly made. Kevin reluctantly stepped forward to grab another chicken then settled back into the chair. This time Kevin was a little more composed, he had learned lessons from his first attempt. This time his hands applied only the necessary pressure and the bird fell silent at Kevin's feet. Curly, his hands shaking, removed the bird from the floor, while Brian was still glued to the wall awaiting his call to play the executioner, fear building up inside him as he watched his older brother become more professional at his task.

A silence filled the basement as Kevin got on with the job, and the two men started feeling a bit uneasy allowing the boys to carry out the task that they were not prepared to do themselves. Brian finally broke the silence, "Why don't you and Curly, have a go Dad, or are you still too scared?"

"Shut up, Brian it's bad enough doing this without listening to you going on. Anyway it will soon be your turn," continued Kevin.

Silence filled the room once again as Kevin got into

the swing of things, but his stomach seemed to be turning in knots, as he did something he thought he would never have to. One by one the chickens fell at his feet until the fifth one was removed by a sheepish looking Curly.

Kevin looked towards his younger brother and Brian looked back at Kevin with eyes wide open, he shouted out. "I'm not killing the other five. Let me Dad do it."

The boys' father chose not to have heard Brian's outburst, hoping they would sort it out themselves. Curly also remained quiet, not wanting to get involved in family matters.

Brian might have been the younger of the two boys by one year, but he had more to say. He accused his father and Curly of being cowards, and the two men looked down at the floor.

"Come on, Brian, its your turn," said Kevin.

"No, let me Dad do it instead of watching us."

"What do you mean I'm the one who is doing it, you haven't killed any of them, and if you don't kill any of them I will keep the ten shillings all for myself."

"Well you can do the rest seeing that you're so good at killing chickens."

"Alright, big mouth, I will but don't expect any of the money," said Kevin, who was by now in full control of what he was doing. "Anyway you're all cowards, me Dad, Curly, and you."

He felt as though he had been cheated in having to do the job all by himself and his stomach still felt funny, but he did not want to lose face in front of the rest of them. So Kevin continued with his grim task until all ten chickens had been slaughtered.

As Kevin got up from the chair, Curly moved forward to hand the money to him for finishing the task. Curly's foot caught the prostrate body of the last chicken to be killed and its twitching form seemed to throw itself at

Curly's leg. He yelled, with terror in his voice and as he collapsed in a heap, the coins fell from his hands and scattered onto the floor of the basement. Kevin rushed forward to pick them up, then, generously handed half of them to his brother. As the two boys looked back from the doorway they smiled as they saw their father struggling to help Curly to his feet.

MARY ANN

Mary Ann looked across the table at Barney filling his pipe with Brown Flake tobacco. She could see the strength in his hands, his pipe was held in his left and his right hand packed the tobacco in tightly. He ripped a piece of paper from the old newspaper that was covering the table as a make-do tablecloth, but was careful not to upset the contents of the pipe. He screwed the strip of paper up and leaned forward to light it from the open fire in the grate.

Barney could see the reflection on the back of his hand from the shining oven door, which was part of the fire range, and he could see the cavity at the side of the oven which allowed the heat from the open fire to warm the inside of the oven for cooking purposes. Barney smiled as he straightened himself in his chair with the lighted paper up to his waiting pipe, and after sucking the air a couple of times, the tobacco gave way to the pressure and ignited.

Sitting in the old Windsor chair was Mary Ann with her elbows on the armrests. She kept looking at the strong hands that held the pipe, wondering how he was going to cope with forced retirement from the sea. Barney was all of five-feet-eight inches in his stocking feet and he still retained the straight back and body of an old sea dog. This was a term he would use when explaining what he did to feed himself and his family. His hair was still fair with just a touch of grey.

She was proud that Barney's friends and family all regarded him as a smart and clean man with a good nature. He had given her three handsome sons and three fine daughters but had not seen much of them because of his time in the Merchant Service. His life was the sea, which he joined in 1899 and now it had been taken away from him in 1943 because somebody in authority felt he was too old at the age of sixty-five. He was born in County Cork and the sea had always influenced his life. His father had been a Marine Engineer, who worked in a Dock Yard, in Passage, but Barney had chosen the sea. Now he felt like a rusting old hulk being towed away to the breaker's yard to finish his life as a redundant sea dog cast up on the banks of the River Mersey.

Mary Ann sat in silence, her eyes downcast, looking at the white apron that covered her black skirt, the hem was down to her ankle and she saw Barney leaning forward, still holding his pipe with his left hand, as he lifted a large piece of coal to throw on the open fire. It gave the room a warm friendly glow in its quest to outdo the dim gas mantle that looked very frail in the holder hanging from the ceiling.

Two large pieces of coal, the tops of which were still black, were starting to split from the heat and little blue flames of gas kept jumping up and down, capturing Barney's attention. Several large gilt-framed photographs hung from the walls of the small square room showing off the sons and daughters of Barney and Mary Ann. The faces in the large photographs seemed to take on a life of their own each time the reflection from the fire flickered across the glass in the frames.

Barney sat back in his old wooden chair, his left hand holding the pipe in his mouth and his right hand cupping his elbow to give it support. Over the rim of his pipe his blue eyes were on Mary Ann, and a steady pall of smoke drifted up towards the ceiling. Barney could see that she was no longer the straight limbed, dark haired girl who had given birth to his children, she had aged much too soon. Barney felt a mixture of remorse and guilt.

'Six months I have been home with her, six months

73

out of forty-four years,' he thought to himself. Most of the time it would be a couple of weeks, then back to sea on the coffee run around the South American Coast, or the River Plate.

They continued to sit in silence, each of them enjoying the warmth of the fire. Barney's eyes were still on Mary Ann, and he thanked God that she was still with him to look after him in his old age. She felt nervous but she was not sure why. Her eyes were still downcast, but she could still see Barney smoking his pipe. It was strange to see him so contented in his chair and she thought, 'at last I have him to myself'. She felt as though time was standing still, yet time was passing them by, the kids had gone, but Polly the parrot was still in her green cage in the corner of the room.

Mary Ann could remember the times Barney would make plans to go home to Cobh, when the kids had grown up but as time went on she knew he felt Liverpool was not for the leaving.

Mary Ann shifted her gaze, Barney's hand seemed to tighten around the pipe. A short puff of smoke took a horizontal course towards the open fire, as his hand lost its grip on the falling pipe, his eyes closed and his head fell forward. Mary Ann fell to her knees. She pushed her head to his chest. Her body went limp, and her tears flowed as she looked up into Barney's face as she held it in her hands. Polly the parrot started to get excited, calling Barney's name, but that was not unusual. Polly always seemed to know when Barney was due home from sea and she would jump about repeating his name many hours before he arrived.

Mary Ann turned her head from Barney, the tears still running down her cheeks. She looked towards Polly in her cage, and the bird looked at Mary Ann, her wings flapping up and down, the way she would when it was

74

too warm, in an effort to try and cool herself; or when she wanted to leave the cage to fly around the small square room, before she would perch on the mantelpiece above the fire. Mary Ann was still on her knees in front of Barney's limp body, wiping the tears from her eyes, reaching out her right hand, which she rubbed on the side of Barney's face.

"You have gone away and left me again, just when I thought I had you to myself."

The bird started to flap her wings again. She was becoming agitated and calling out Barney's name.

"For God's sake be quiet will ya. You always knew when he was due home, you would jump up and down and now, damn ya, and you know he's gone."

Mary Ann stood up and turned to the cage, leaned over and pulled the folded blanket that lay at the back of it over Polly. She then turned to face Barney's sagging body in the chair. She put her right hand at Barney's back and her left hand under his knees and pulled his body onto the floor. She then spread out an old blanket alongside the body and rolled him over onto it, straightening his legs and arms. She brought a large bowl of water from the kitchen and placed it next to Barney's body. She stripped the clothes off him, folding them in a neat pile on the table, and about washing his body, while kneeling on the blanket. Mary Ann's mind was spinning as she continued to wash the prostrate corpse of Barney.

"How many times have I washed my babies like this and now I'm doing the same to you but I won't be putting you to bed like I did with my children. Soon they will come and take you away from me and all I will be left with are my memories."

She finished washing the body and covered it with the remains of the blanket, she then pulled herself up onto her Windsor chair to gain strength before her family arrived on the scene.

'There's work to be done,' she thought to herself, as she looked down at the laid out body of Barney.

Mary Ann died a few months later of a broken heart, as did Polly.

THE SEAFARER'S WIFE

To the memory of Mary Ann

Two score years and four to work my
Bones, sit and think in fading light,
Lie alone on a damp cold night dream the
Dreams that never begin.

Shadow on the wall in the flickering light,
Hand on the cot beside the bed, the river is
Still on a foggy night, the clang of the
Buoy as it moves with the tide.

Where is my dream on oceans wide you
Have left me to push alone in the night,
Cry out in pain in the stillness of dawn, no
Hand on my cheek to comfort me.

A vision of you as the stars in the night,
You are here for a moment to warm my
Heart, forsake the sea, my body grows
Weak, the days are long

The ebbing tides with the children have
Fled, you comfort me now, in perfect bliss
For only one summer and autumn, and
Then you leave me, with only my dreams.

CORDUROY PANTS AND KHAKI SHIRTS

It was a quiet Friday morning in 1978 and Joey was making his way to the Pier Head for a cup of tea. The Dock Road was quiet, the traffic had not built up, the speedometer on his hackney cab showed twenty-seven miles an hour, which gave him time to look around. 'God, it's changed,' he thought to himself. The early sunshine had pushed its way through the windscreen of the cab and onto Joey's weather-beaten face, and he could feel the warmth of the sun descend deep into his body. 'It's good to be alive,' he thought. Joey's mind kept drifting back. 'It's funny the way life goes, I can still remember walking along this road when I was just a kid looking at all of the ships and imagining the romance of sailing away in them. God, I soon found out it was more hard work, and little romance.'

A smile spread across his face, as he thought it had not been a bad life, sailing the seven seas. Now it was all gone, there were just empty docks and scrap yards. What a future to give the kids! The sight of the Liver Birds in the distance snapped Joey out of his thoughts. The cab radio was on low and giving out information. 'I hope they don't want me to pick anybody up until I've had a cuppa.' The hackney cab swung its way to the right at the traffic lights past the Liver Building and onto the big plateau, in front of the large Pier Head buildings. He was about to get out of his taxi when a grating voice came over the well-worn, crackling radio.

"Anybody in town, or by the Pier Head?"

"Delta One calling, I'm at the Pier Head," said Joey.

"Go to Lime Street Station, pick up Mr. Brady," said the operator at the other end of the radio.

'Well, there goes my cuppa. God knows when I will get one now,' thought Joey. He made his way to Liverpool's main line station; 'I hope it's a good fare and not just going around the corner,' he thought. The cab pulled its way into the station.

"Are you Mr. Brady?"

"Yes, we want to go to Esk Street Police Station," came a nervous reply. Mr. Brady was holding a pretty little girl of about eighteen months and standing next to him was another little girl, three years old and a young woman, who looked small and frail. Mr. Brady put the children in first, then he gently put his hand on the young woman's shoulder, like a shepherd guiding sheep into the security of his pen. The strain of travelling showed in her movements as he helped her into the taxi cab.

Mr. Brady leaned forward, "Do you know Esk Street Police Station?" he asked, speaking with a Northern Irish accent.

Joey nodded his head.

"I was told that it was down by the docks."

"Yes, that's right," replied Joey.

A half-smile came to Joey's face, when he felt the strange feeling in his stomach. 'Yes, I know Esk Street Police Station,' he thought to himself.

"We have been travelling since early this morning. We set off from home in Ipswich at one o'clock last night," said Mr. Brady.

"I see," said Joey, looking at the young couple and the children through his rear view mirror.

The young woman had her arms around the two children, her face said many things; she seemed as though she wanted to burst into tears, but he could see the restraint in her face, so as not to alarm the children. The young man wanted to talk and he could see that Joey was a good listener; Joey had that sort of face, although his passengers could only see one side of it, as he half-turned his head to them.

The young man leaned forward in his seat at the back of the cab, his hands held together. Joey could see him in the mirror, having lost all composure.

"All our money is gone in paying our train fare, and the taxis as well. We had to borrow money off the neighbours, but the Police are paying our fare when we get to the boat. They told us last night that my wife's mother has been hurt and we don't know how she is." The pain they were suffering was flowing out of them.

"We don't know what it will be like when we get to Belfast," said the young wife, her arms pulling her children in closer to her.

Joey felt very uneasy listening to the young couple, and he felt for them. Joey had now lost interest in wondering if it was to be a good fare in the back of his cab. His only concern was for the young family in his charge, though it was only for a few minutes. The strange feeling came back in his stomach as he thought about Esk Street Police Station. Joey could not have been much older than the little three years old. His own family had been in despair like so many of the people in his community who lived in the area around Esk Street and his mind was racing back, pushing away the mist of time to reveal the memories of his childhood, in particular.

He remembered the heavy, green door and the big brass tap in the Police Station yard. He could see his mother holding his hand while she stood in a queue of women and children in the police yard. It was warm inside and the lights were bright, unlike the gas lamp in his home. Joey could see the folding tables in straight lines and well-dressed ladies standing at the other side of the tables, with lots of clothes in a big heap. Sitting on the floor were children trying on pairs of clogs. The boys were given corduroy pants and khaki shirts and the girls were given a blouse and skirt made of similar material. Joey sat next to the rest of the kids waiting for his turn to receive clothes from the Police Benevolent Fund.

"Have you got your ticket?" said one of the well-dressed ladies. His mother pushed the ticket forward on the table and the ladies of charity dished out their wares.

Joey again looked back in his rear view mirror.

"The children have not eaten since last night. They have slept most of the journey," said Mrs. Brady, her eyes downcast, her arms still protecting her children as she held them close to her. The little family fell silent for the remainder of the journey.

Joey walked into the police station yard, its large green wooden door drawn back to the inside of the stone wall, the large brass tap still protruding from the wall. Joey smiled as he thought about the times he and his brothers stood with buckets and bowls in their hands, along with dozens of other people waiting their turn to collect water from the big brass tap. Joey could remember his mother turning the tap in the hovel where they lived and the water failing to appear. Joey never knew why the water dried up, but when it did, out would come buckets and off he would go to Esk Street Police Station. Joey rubbed his hand over the grey Yorkshire stone of the building as he walked towards the main entrance.

Mr. Brady and his little family followed, tired and weary. Mr. Brady led the way up the three steps leading to the reception area, carrying what little possessions they had. Joey offered to take some of them, but Mr. Brady declined. He also carried the baby while his frail wife walked in behind him with their other child. A Police Sergeant stood behind the mahogany topped desk, his large hands lying flat on the polished wood. He was a big man with the round, weather-beaten face of a middle aged man, giving off a friendly smile that radiated from his blue eyes. His hair was wavy, and going grey.

'The lights were still bright,' thought Joey, although it was a fine summer day. The lack of windows necessitated them being on for twenty-four hours a day.

"Are you Mr. Brady?" said the Sergeant, before Joey could introduce the family. The Sergeant lifted the heavy flap of the desk and came around to the front.

"I suppose you're hungry," he said, looking at Mrs. Brady. "Well, we will soon put a stop to that" he said, taking an interest in them. The Sergeant offered his hand to the oldest child. "I've got the kettle on," he continued.

Joey walked into the kitchen with the Bradys. A strong smell of bacon filled the air.

"Sit yourselves down, we will soon get things moving and it won't be long before we get you down to the boat."

Joey looked at the Sergeant, who had his back to him, preparing a breakfast for Mr. Brady and his family, and towards Mrs. Brady, sitting on the wooden bench, beside the plastic top table her two children clinging to her. The scene before Joey filled him with emotions and memories so intertwined that he was not sure whether he should shout for joy or burst out crying.

The Police Station was the last remnant of the community Joey had grown up in. The families he knew had been scattered to the winds. His emotions were coming from the pit of his stomach. He wanted to shake the hand of the Sergeant, who still had his back to him, but he knew it would make him look foolish, for how could the Sergeant and the Brady family possibly understand what he was feeling?

"I will have to go now, Mr. Brady. I wish you well on your journey," said Joey glancing towards Mrs. Brady and her two children.

"Thanks, Sarge," said Joey, walking out of the kitchen

and into the station yard, once again rubbing his hands over the Yorkshire stone.

Joey made his way to the Pier Head for the belated cup of tea. The radio was silent in his cab. Joey was much calmer as he sat watching the children feeding the pigeons on the Pier Head's Plateau, with his long-awaited cup of tea.

PRAYERS BEFORE WORK

Terry and George arrived at the construction site over-burdened with their carpenter's tools in one hand and a well used suitcase in the other. The bus journey from Reading Station to the site at Burfield was a miserable experience for them, made worse because they had no idea just what to expect. They had no written contract as they just had to take the chance that the job they had been promised would be there when they arrived on a cold February day in 1956. Another worry would be their sleeping arrangements for the night.

The conditions on the site, miles out into the countryside of Berkshire were very primitive. Hundreds of men worked up to their knees in mud, without a canteen or any other welfare facility. Toilet facilities were so bad that it was more hygienic to take a shovel and find a quiet spot in a field. The management had no regard whatsoever for the lives of those they employed. Every day men would be sent inside concrete bunkers to strip away the steel plates, which held the newly formed concrete roof in place. They knew that men were at risk carrying out this work because the concrete had only been poured in less than twenty-four hours earlier with perhaps not enough time to set.

The living conditions for most of the men were not fit for a wild animal to live in. Any change would have been difficult due to Trade Union officials being about as rare as caviar in a working man's canteen. The management had provided an ex-army camp a couple of miles down the road from the site for their accommodation. The bunk beds were just about acceptable, but the food was lousy. Men on the Burfield site in Berkshire had come from almost every part of the British Isles. They had travelled not because they were seeking adventure, or to enjoy a different way of life, but because they had been driven there by economic factors beyond their control. Very little at that time had changed in the building industry since the publication of Robert Tressall's book, *The Ragged Trousered Philanthropists* in 1914, describing the terrible working conditions of building workers.

Terry moved about the scaffolding, fixing into place the heavy timber. 1956 was not a prosperous year, so Terry had left his wife and baby daughter in Newcastle and travelled south, with George, to find work. Like the rest of the carpenters, Terry would finish his section of formwork each day, ready for the concrete to be poured in and so it went on. Terry stood about five feet ten inches with a handsome face, and a dark complexion, his shoulders and legs were strong, his waist slim. Nature had been kind to Terry and it had brought him to full maturity at the age of twenty-two. He was a quiet young man more suited to the Church, who was never heard to use swear words. George was a happy go-lucky young man but a very disciplined tradesman, who stood about the same height as Terry.

At the end of each day, buses provided by the company, would take the men back to the camp. Hundreds of workers were herded into long dormitories. Tradesmen like Terry and George slept four men to a room. The only comfort that most of them could look forward to was to be found in the local pubs and bars around the area which became overcrowded. There were times when prejudice was displayed by local landlords as if one had any accent other than a southern one, there was the risk of being asked to "drink up and get out," though there was of course safety in numbers. Later, it would be the long walk back to the camp, to collapse on their bunks and think about family back home, until, eventually, exhausted sleep would overtake them.

Every morning Terry would be out of bed an hour before his workmates, as he was an early riser. He would be first in the canteen and then he would wander off to the little Church, down the road a mile from the camp, but he would always be ready to board the bus at the appointed time for the ride to the construction site. The buses would pull into the compound alongside the main gates, and the men would file through them to clock-on at eight o'clock. Terry and George would soon be in position on the scaffolding, stripping out the timber formwork from the concrete, which, hopefully, had set. Most of the men were engaged in the same operation, while the rest would be in the fields digging trenches and laying pipes.

About a hundred yards away from Terry and George was another young carpenter working on a different section of the job. He was a fine big lad, not unlike Terry in build, but this fellow was about six-foot-one tall. He had a good head of fair hair and a strong face but it had a darkness that seemed to portray an angry young man. Just like the rest of them he had arrived from another part of the country but, unlike most of his comrades, he cared little for work. He would often be seen walking about his section of the job making a nuisance of himself, and he had become known as the Scowler. Terry, because of his quiet manner, was easy prey for him.

"Hey, Geordie, have you been to Church this morning? I suppose it helps you work better."

The taunts would go on until his voice would disappear into the next section of the job, where he would cause further trouble. Sensible men hold their tongues on a construction site, except when seeking better pay and working conditions from the management, but this lad had become a pain in the neck. He was a bully and he had found the quiet Terry an easy target. Terry spoke to few people because he was happy to let George do his talking. Those men who were close to him knew that he only lived for his little family in Newcastle, where he would rather have stayed. George had become one of the Shop Stewards trying to arrange the welfare facilities and was returning to the section that he was working on, when one of the men shouted to him, "He's been at it again."

He was informed that Terry had been suffering more abuse from his tormentor, and that things had come to a head.

"They're going to settle it once and for all", said some of the men.

How would Terry fare, George wondered, being involved in a physical encounter with this very strong tall young man of over six-foot. George feared for Terry's safety as he imagined the outcome of the intended fight. During the course of the day, this incident left George's mind due to the pressure of work and the Trade Union problems. At five o'clock, the end of the working day, George made his way to book off with the rest of the men through the slime and mud to the site office to put his card in the clocking machine.

George, by this time, had let the incident concerning his friend slip to the back of his mind. Just beyond the site office and the high fence, lay the huge compound where the buses parked ready to take the men back to the camp at the end of the working day. As George went through the gate he was astonished to see hundreds of men who had formed themselves into a huge circle. The scene reminded him of something he had read about. 'Yes that's it,' he thought, 'the Yukon in the days of the Gold Rush where men would stand in their hundreds watching two gold miners proving themselves to their eager audience.'

The reasons for the confrontation no longer mattered,

only that two men were defending their honour, standing bare-knuckled and toe-to-toe, unconsciously using the Queensbury Rules. Those in the audience who knew the two protagonists saw only two human beings doing battle with their fists. One no longer looked at the Scowler as a big mouthed bully, or at the Newcastle man as a quietly spoken, good Catholic boy. There was only admiration for the way the pair conducted themselves during a raw challenge.

The fight between the two men became more intense as the punches were crisp and solid, but it was Terry's punches that were landing on the target area with sickening precision. The Scowler's face started to resemble a battered tomato. As the battle continued, neither man showed signs of going down and the longer they fought, the greater grew the admiration of the crowd. Their heads were used only for thinking while with their feet they tried to avoid blows, as their hands did the fighting.

Watching the battle unfold before him, George became uneasy and concerned. He realised that he was supposed to improve conditions for his fellow workers and not stand by watching them beat one another. He was thinking to himself, 'I was supposed to settle any problems that the men had with the management and this was another problem.' Slowly George walked over to the two men and hoped that those watching would not think he was taking the part of one of the two protagonists. George pushed his way between the two gladiators saying, "Right finish, no more. The fight's over," and so the battle ended.

Some would say the spectacle was raw, crude, uncivilized. Yet those same people could admire the use of a sharp steel cutlass slicing a fellow human being in half and justify this action as being a necessary evil in times of war. Many would condemn this fight as an act of brutality, yet respect those with the viper's tongue destroying a man with character assassination to satisfy their own lust and greed for power. Nevertheless, the two men who George witnessed doing battle in a field were civilized enough to settle their differences over a pint of beer at the end of the confrontation. The living and working conditions created a breeding ground for inadequacies prevalent in some men.

On a rare weekend break the following day, the young Scowler had to meet his girlfriend in London. She would see with horror his badly bruised face. Meanwhile, a smile would descend on the managers on the Burfield site. They were the only winners in any confrontation, which occurred between men whose only reason for being on building sites like Burfield was to scratch out a living for their families.

TOM'S BIG DAY

Tom was seated along with his fellow graduates in the front rows of the stalls, while waiting for the second of nine graduation ceremonies to begin.

For a few seconds his mind wandered back to the day he gave up his job in the motor trade, secure but poorly paid, and all the dead-end jobs he had tried since leaving school at the age of fifteen. It seemed only yesterday, rather than five years ago, since he had gone to Harlech College in Wales to join a hundred or more mature students, who were all keen to obtain a Diploma in Higher Education. He thought about the friends made during the two years there, but they had scattered to the wind. Only a few friendships had survived, and they would remain for the rest of his life, along with those made during his three years at Liverpool University, where he had just obtained his 1st Class B.A. Honours Degree.

Everyone stood as a blast from the organ announced the arrival of the processions, led by ushers in their blue robes. Representatives of the students, staff, and dignitaries were mainly in black or red gowns, adding to the splendour of the occasion. The final procession was led by the Esquire Bedell, carrying the University Mace, bringing in the Chancellor with his train proudly supported by a smart pageboy, the young son of a member of staff, who fitted the black velvet suit.

The Chancellor congratulated the graduates and spoke of the value of learning, quoting Shakespeare, which had a profound effect on Tom. The Public Orator then came to the rostrum to introduce the two Honorary Graduates, and one of them made a speech of acceptance, in reply. The Dean then stepped forward to read out the names of those from the Faculty to be introduced to the Chancellor, for the conferment of degrees.

At last it was Tom's turn to mount the few stairs onto the stage, shake hands with the Chancellor, and receive his graduation certificate on stepping down.

The Philharmonic Hall was the scene for this splendid spectacle, and Tom was highly impressed by the décor. His thoughts turned to a time when he was young and his mother, Bunny, had brought him here to a concert. A soloist had sat at the piano playing *Moonlight Sonata* and Tom now felt he could almost hear that wonderful music drifting through the Hall. He remembered his mother telling him of the time when she was a young girl herself, and how she had fallen in love with that same piece of music by Beethoven. Her grandmother had taken her to the cinema to see *Dangerous Moonlight* in the early days of the Second World War, and it was the theme song of the film.

When the majestic ceremony was over, Tom enjoyed the bright summer's day as he strolled with his mother and grandfather to the nearby beautiful University Abercromby Gardens, before going back to his department for the celebration cheese and wine party. Tom could feel the solid but gentle frame of his mother as he had her arm in his, with his other arm supporting his frail grandfather. He thought about the time those shoulders were strong from working as a gardener for the Council. Grandad had not asked too much from his labours; just being able to give a service to the community was all that he had needed. Tom could remember him when his back was straight, and his limbs firm. He knew that the gifts he had received from his family that were passed down in the genes through reproduction, were far greater than all the material things in life.

Bunny gently took her father's arm and pointed to an

empty seat by the Victorian railings, and led him over to have a rest after their walk. They stayed for a while enjoying the sunshine, both so proud of Tom, who was tall, and his mother only two or three inches shorter than him. She was fifty-eight, but retained the fine figure of a woman twenty years her junior. Her hair was still fair and the years of discipline and dedication as a professional dancer had rewarded her with good health and a youthful figure.

No sooner had the old man sat down than one of Tom's friends came across to take their photo and also one of Tom with his mother. Bunny wondered if she should join her father on the seat and allow another of Tom's friends to stand by his side, but her son insisted she remain where she was. She kept looking at him proudly and only turned away when asked to face the camera, which captured the gentle smile on her face.

However, the camera could not see into her mind as it roamed down the years to a time in her life when she was at crossroads; a young widowed mother with a tiny baby, wondering what the future would hold. She remembered thinking about the wise decisions she had to make, right for both of them. Bunny had watched Tom grow from the helpless infant in the early years; from the foal with uncertain legs to the stallion, firm and strong. Yes, she could remember the times he had looked back at her with uncertainty in his eyes as he moved further away to explore the world about him. Bunny was well aware that she could only guide him while he remained within the confines of her own influence. She remembered the doubts and fears that she experienced over the years. Now her son had mastered the art of coping with the world she had brought him into. She was so glad to be the mother of this fine young man.

Looking away from the camera towards the bench,

she saw her father, Tom Senior, who had stoked up his pipe and was contentedly puffing away on it. She could see he was relaxed, at peace with the world, sitting there with the gentle rays of sunshine falling on his face. This was, in fact, one of the happiest days of his life. His mind was not only on Tom and his daughter but also on the streets they had walked along, surprised that so many of the buildings had been swallowed up to become part of the University campus.

Bunny could also see his smile, which came from his eyes. Words did not have to pass between them. They were both happy knowing that Tom had at last achieved his ambition and had a job waiting for him as a social worker.

THE CONFESSION

Brendon walked into the Church with the guilt of a condemned man waiting to come face to face with his executioner and, almost on tiptoe, advanced towards the pews by the confessional box. From the corner of his eye he could see two elderly ladies, a young man, and a boy who went to the same school as himself. They were all waiting to have their confessions heard. Brendon sat down in an empty pew, ready for his turn.

Time seemed to stand still for him as those in front of him disappeared one at a time into the confessional box. He heard the door click each time they went in, and listened for the gentle thud of the lock bolt every time they came out. Brendon looked at them all as each one of them knelt down for their act of contrition, asking forgiveness.

'Their sins could not be as big as mine,' Brendon kept repeating to himself. He waited for the thud of the confessional box door as, at last, his fellow pupil came out. The sound, though low pitched, reverberated around the almost empty Church as Brendon pulled himself to his feet, and walked towards the solid oak door of the dimly lit cubical. The darkness heightened the fear that was in his mind as he sat down beside the partition that separated him from his parish priest. Brendon could see the outline of the priest's head and shoulders as he stared into the screen. He was gripped with the thoughts of the unknown as the words came tumbling out.

"Bless me I have sinned," muttered Brendon, with eyes closed.

"Can we start again, and do it right this time?" was the reply.

"Bless me Father for I have sinned."

"That's better, now let's go on," said the priest, sensing Brendon's state of mind.

"I used swear words seven times this week and I was cheeky to me Mam. I kicked next door's cat because it was crying on the windowsill all night, I had a whiff of Peggy Kehoe's cigarette and I was late for school yesterday because I never wanted to go. I was fighting with the lad next door because he tried to take my sweets and I never went to Church on Sunday, Father."

"Why did you not come to Church?" asked the priest, in a low gentle voice.

"Because …"

"Because what?" queried the priest.

"Well … well, it was the moneylender," replied Brendon.

"What moneylender, what are you trying to tell me, my son?" The priest's voice was still low as he encouraged Brendon to continue.

"Father, she died on Saturday and I killed her." said Brendon, each word coming in rapid succession.

"I see, so you killed this woman, who died on Saturday?" The priest's voice was still low and encouraging. "Are you certain that you carried out this terrible deed?"

"Yes, Father" said the panic stricken voice of Brendon.

"Tell me my son, how old are you?"

"I'm ten, Father."

"You're ten years old and you killed the moneylender who died on Saturday? Well I think we should start from the beginning, just take your time and tell me what happened," requested the priest.

"Father, it was my bad thoughts that did it."

"You had bad thoughts and then she died! Did you not like this woman, and do you think that is the reason why she died?" queried the priest.

"Yes Father, I wanted her to die and she did," replied

Brendon, the nervous tension rising in the boy's voice.

"Why did you want this woman to die?" asked the priest.

"Because she was a money lender, Father."

"Is that all, so you hoped she would die. What harm had she done to you that you should have such wicked thoughts?" he asked, gently as the boy was still troubled.

"She took all me Mam's money every week, Father and I would see me Mam cry because she had none."

"Where is your Dad? Is he at home?" asked the priest.

"No Father, he is at sea. Me Mam said he is brave because he is in the Merchant Navy," said Brendon. The priest sensed a proud boast from Brendon when he talked about his Dad.

"Tell me, what is the name of this woman who took all your mother's money each week and where did she live?" said the priest.

"Her name is Mrs. Cranley and she lived in our street, Father," answered Brendon.

"Did the other neighbours borrow money from her?" asked the priest.

"Yes Father," replied Brendon.

"Do you think that they have wicked thoughts about her because she was a moneylender?" asked the priest.

"I don't know, Father," was the boy's answer.

"So do you think perhaps you might have been the only person to wish to do this woman some harm?" said the priest, his voice still low, not wanting to panic Brendon.

"I never did her any harm, Father," replied Brendon,

"But you did have wicked thoughts about this woman, that's a way of harming people isn't it?" asked the priest.

Brendon fell silent for a few seconds as he shifted himself on the hard wooden seat.

"But I never wanted to kill her. I just wanted to stop her taking me Mam's money. She put it into a big bag that had lots of other money in it and sometimes she would count it. While she was doing that she would have a sickly grin on her face, and she would glare at me over the top of her specs looking like an old crow. Well that's what me Gran said."

"Now don't you think that it's wicked describing the woman as an old crow," suggested the priest.

"Well me Gran thinks she is, Father."

"I won't argue with you over that, but it's still wrong of you to think that way."

"Yes Father."

"How many brothers and sisters do you have?" asked the priest.

"Three sisters and five brothers Father, well there's four brothers and me, that makes five lads, and our Mary, Kathleen and Rosie," replied Brendon, counting them on his fingers, while wriggling about on the wooden seat.

"I don't need to know the names of your brothers and sisters. I'm quite sure that your bad thoughts, as wicked as they were towards this woman, could not have been the cause of her death. Do you understand what I am saying to you?" continued the priest.

"Yes, Father." answered Brendon.

"Now go and say three 'Hail Mary's,' two 'Our Father's, and then say a prayer for the repose of Mrs. Cranley's immortal soul and God will forgive you for your sin of bad thoughts, providing you have no more of them," said the priest.

"Thank you, Father." muttered Brendon gratefully as he stumbled out, glad to have been let off so lightly.

MY DILEMMA

I arrived in Dublin on a half hour flight from Liverpool at about nine o'clock on a Tuesday morning intending to stay for three days, it was a last minute decision. However I never gave a thought to booking some sort of accommodation in advance because I felt that this would not be a problem, as I would soon find a place of sanctuary. When I arrived in the city however I had a rude awakening, as tourists were everywhere, and then I realized it was the busy first week in August. I made my way to Bewley's Café in Westmoreland Street for a bite to eat and to do a little thinking.

After eating, my energy level was raised somewhat and my task was to find somewhere to stay. This however proved to be no easy matter and to add to my anxiety it had started to rain, just as I stepped out onto the pavement. It continued like a spluttering, dripping tap, as I made my way in search for accommodation and the more I walked, the more the tap seemed to be turned on. I am nothing, if not well prepared when I go away for a few days, with my little shoulder bag containing a clean shirt, a pair of underpants, one pair of socks and a toothbrush. I did not have an umbrella or cap so the dancing rain played a rhythm on my bald head.

I was starting to look a sorry sight in my quest to find a bed for the night. I tried a number of places, even the youth hostels, but the answer was always the same, "Sorry, we're full up." Not being in the big league, I could not afford the price of one of the larger hotels even if a room was available. I was getting to the stage where paranoia was setting in, but then, some of my friends say I am that way already and I suppose I have to face the fact that I must be out of my head; for who in his right mind would go to Dublin the first week in August without making arrangements for somewhere to stay. At last I thought, 'I'm in luck,' as I came across a small hotel with a sign in the window, which read 'Vacancies.'

I walked to the main entrance, but a glass door blocked my way so I rang the bell. It attracted the attention of a pleasant looking young woman who I could see coming to the door. I wondered if I had cracked it and if this young woman was going to say, "yes, we have a room." She turned the key on her side of the door and a smile greeted me, which I returned ready to move forward, my mouth opened about to plead for sanctuary, but the young woman got in first.

"Sorry, but we are full up."

"But the sign," I stuttered.

"Oh yes," she continued, "I forgot to take it down."

The smile was still on her face, and I turned to leave as the excuses kept coming from her lips my paranoia was starting to build up, and off I went feeling very sorry for myself. Then out of the clear sky came the sunshine, the rain had gone and across the street in big bold letters I saw, 'Barry's Hotel.' I ran towards it, well, not quite ran but I certainly quickened my pace.

"Have you got a room for three nights?" I asked the young woman who looked up at me from behind the desk, not a smile on her face.

"Yes, we can let you have a room on the first floor, en suite."

I accepted the offer and went straight upstairs and unpacked my bag, taking out my sparse belongings, then lay back on the bed, thankful that I had my own bathroom. 'Good old Dublin, I knew you wouldn't let me down,' I thought to myself, as the paranoia was subsiding. Well, now that I was certain of a roof over my head I felt secure.

It was a nice thought that I would not be looking up at the stars from lying on a park bench, so I set off for a walk down O'Connell Street and once more made for Bewley's Café to sit in wonderment at all the people who keep that café busy all day long. It is very much a place to have a cuppa or a meal because of its wonderful ambience, young and old alike love to sit in its world of charm. After my meal, I set out for The Dublin Writers Museum and what a joy it was. I felt like a peeping Tom looking through a window into the private world of those wonderful Irish writers. Then I don't suppose there is such a place as a private world for a writer. If I was an intruder into their personal lives, at least I know a little more about them.

James Joyce, that all embracing artist, for example whose words strike out at you and hold you in their embrace, like Michelangelo's images. Sean O'Casey is another favourite writer for many people and Liam O'Flaherty, but the darling of them all is Brendan Behan. Maybe it is because of his working class background, although some have tried to dispute his early upbringing. Behan, a Dublin man, had after all a brief encounter with another town I love so well, Liverpool.

Then after taking in all this intellectual nourishment at the museum, I decided to sample the flavour of the local pubs. The following morning after a good night's sleep, I joined the thousands of tourists who had come to old Dublin City. It was a bright and sunny day and everybody seemed to be in a happy mood, no one more so than myself because the joyous atmosphere had put a spring in my step and my legs felt as if they were free from the worry of searching for a room the previous night. I thought I would go and look at the fruit market at the back of O'Connell Street, but first I had to enter Henry Street, and join the hundreds of shoppers who filled this pedestrian highway.

I had the feeling I was on a large chessboard, which

was the length and width of the street with too many chess pieces so there was nowhere to move. I was there too, a pawn, only too happy to take part in this crazy game. A move could only take place when somebody stepped sideways or if they disappeared into one of the many shops that ran the full length of the street. It was great to wander from one side to the other, space permitting of course, without worrying about motorcars tearing past. In many ways it was a nice feeling to be pushed by a large mass of people, and at one stage, my mind took me into another dimension as I ploughed my way along the street, and I seemed now to be taking part in a gigantic musical.

The buskers lined each side of the thoroughfare, playing everything from classical to pop music, and all waiting their cue from the Director before everyone burst into song. To the right of me was Moore Street, housing the fruit and fish stalls. The whole area was filled with people buying and selling, and many of the women selling their goods were full of a wonderful sense of humour. This is needed for them to survive in the winter months; however, this was summertime and the air was filled with laughter, even though money was hard to come by.

Molly Malone will never be dead or, *die of the fever*, as the song goes, while those women remain at the entrance to Moore Street pushing their old battered prams with a wooden tray on top, displaying a variety of wares; anything from oranges and lemons, to whatever else they could to sell to keep body and soul together. The whole of this area was a cavalcade of colour, a kaleidoscope of people, the good, the bad, the mighty and the poor. This great open-air theatre goes on for six days a week, only coming to rest on a Sunday, when the lights are turned down and silence hits the stage.

I left Henry Street with Moore Street behind me, taking no more part in this ceaseless show and made my way to the nearest café for a much needed cup of coffee, a bacon buttie and a chance to rest my weary feet. After this, I stepped out once more into the milling crowd of tourists, who, like myself, never seemed to know where they were going. After strolling for some time in the sunshine, amusing myself by looking at the tourists in Grafton Street, I made my way to the Abbey Theatre where the name George Bernard Shaw was displayed, which stopped me in my tracks. I stood taking in all the information on the posters, hanging on to every word, much the same way I did when I was a teenager.

The last time I saw a play by the great man himself it was *John Bull's Other Island* at the Gaiety Theatre, Dublin, many years earlier, so I thought I would treat myself once more. The young male attendant at the booking office said he had a seat in the front stalls close to the stage. Somehow I had the feeling that he thought I was a bit deaf. Well, of course he was right, my years working in the shipyard had taken its toll. I smiled at him.

"Yes, that will do me fine, a seat near the stage."

"Please try to be early. The performance starts at eight o'clock prompt," requested the young man.

Walking back towards O'Connell Street clutching my ticket, I felt like a man who had just won a fortune at the local bingo hall. So to celebrate, I made for the first bar that came in sight before I set out for my digs to prepare myself for my night of culture. After quenching my thirst, I left the bar, but on the way out I caught my wristwatch strap on the door and my watch went flying across the pavement. As it was only a cheap battery driven one, I picked up the scattered pieces and put them in the nearest rubbish bin.

In my haste to get ready, I turned on the television in my room to get the time, and the digital clock on the screen showed that I had better put a move on, so off I went at fifteen minutes past seven according to the time on the television screen. Making sure I still had my precious theatre ticket in my pocket, I jumped onto the first bus that came along. I asked the driver if he went anywhere near the Abbey Theatre. He nodded in a sort of polite way without looking at me, and said, "I'll give you a shout where to get off." I then placed the bus fare on the tray in front of the driver, but he refused to take the money. I accepted his kindness gratefully and took a seat thinking that this was a nice way to start an evening at the theatre.

When I arrived at the Abbey, an attendant was standing at the main entrance and I asked him if the bar was open, as I felt like having an orange juice before taking my seat in the auditorium. He looked at me the way you look at an idiot, when they ask you a question for which you have no answer. I moved forward towards the foyer while I was waiting for his answer, but he stopped me in my tracks.

"The bar is closed until seven o'clock," he said, trying to hide a grin.

Then I thought. 'What time must it be now?' I did not have the nerve to ask him. To calm myself down, and to regain my composure, I headed for a bar along the street and ordered a whisky to steady my nerves and, hopefully wipe away the foolish look on my face. When the barman placed the whisky in front of me, I asked him in the most casual way I could, if he would tell me the right time.

"It's forty-five minutes past four o'clock," he replied. I just kept repeating this to myself in disbelief. I thought it priceless that I had arrived more than three hours too early for the performance. What a dilemma I had created for myself, and to think I was going to see George Bernard Shaw's, *The Doctor's Dilemma*!

THE GIFT OF ELOQUENCE

We never planned to go to Ballydaly, three miles outside of Millstreet in West Cork. It just came out of the blue. It was Janet our neighbour, who had booked this little cottage in West Cork and was unable to take advantage of spending two weeks there due to unforeseen family matters. So there we were, Pauline, Katy, Peter and I, making plans for our trip on the ferry *Leinster*, sailing from Liverpool to Dublin. We arrived in Dublin at 7.30 a.m. on the Saturday, ready for our drive in my old car, a 1975 Triumph Toledo, in the hope that it would make it to West Cork, without us having to get out and push. After many hours on the road we arrived and saw the bungalow facing us at the top end of a field.

The entrance was along a narrow path, just wide enough for a car or a tractor. On sight of the bungalow, Katy said, "That can't be it, its too nice." But sure enough it was for us. Mrs. O'Brien, the owner, showed us around the place. She was a pleasant lady with the sort of West Cork accent that makes you feel at ease. Before leaving, she told us to give her a call any time if we were in need of anything, as she lived in a farmhouse at the back of our bungalow. The children, Peter and Katy, soon made friends with two little dogs who lived on the farm.

After a wash and a bite to eat, we all went into the town of Millstreet. While Pauline and the kids did some shopping I took advantage of the local hostelry. We did not stay too long as we were all a little weary after travelling, so we were soon back down the three mile road to Ballydaly and our little bungalow. The next day Sunday, we had a lie-in until 10.30 a.m. and Peter came into the kitchen with two pints of fresh milk, delivered by our landlady's thirteen-year-old son.

By 11.30 a.m. we had finished our breakfast and we then set off for Millstreet, arriving midday. Just on entering the town there is a library and car park on the left, and a general shop and garage on the right, with farm machinery and tractors outside waiting for repair. We parked the car and made our way onto the High Street, just in time to see a procession through the town with the lone piper in the lead. It was then I realized this was the feast of Corpus Christi, so we decided to join them in the service.

After we left the Church, which had been packed to the doors, we did some shopping in the High Street supermarket, then returned to our bungalow and some dinner. About 3 p.m. we set out for Killarney in County Kerry for a couple of hours. Peter was glued to the television and so declined the chance of seeing more of West Cork or Kerry, that afternoon. Pauline, Katy and I started on the seventeen-mile journey.

Everywhere we looked we saw beauty, with Katy repeatedly pointing out everything of interest. On the hillsides just up from the road, we could see new bungalows and others under construction. They were not clustered together, but dotted around the hillsides, just like the old cottages. We were so engrossed in what we saw on our journey that Killarney soon loomed up on the horizon. We walked around the town as though we were on a reconnaissance mission, finding out about all the things we could do and see on our return later in the week.

The following day was a lazy one, because we decided to stay locally and have a look at the scenery in the Ballydaly area. We all had a stroll just below our little house down to the stream, which had a narrow road bridge running over it. The very sight of this clear water coming down from the Derrnassaggart Mountains and separating our little piece of West Cork from County Kerry, was enough for the kids to climb down the bank, strip off their socks and shoes and wade into the water. In pursuit were the two local dogs who had now adopted us during our stay.

The following day we returned to Killarney, with a firm plan drawn up by the children. Who decided that we would hire a pushbike each, at a charge of £2.50 per machine for twenty-four hours, not that we would be in the saddle for twenty-four hours! Fitting ourselves out with bikes was great fun, with a large frame for myself, a lady's bike for Pauline, while Katy decided on a gent's one. Peter tried out every machine in the shop, but at last and a little reluctantly he chose a smaller bike. So off we went, a little shaky at first for the two and a half miles to the Lakes of Killarney.

If you want to see the lakes and you have the energy, I can assure you this is the way to do it, as it was so much easier to navigate the nature trails around the lakes. By the time we arrived, Pauline and I, but not the kids, were a little saddle sore. It was just as well we had the bikes, We came upon Muckross Abbey founded in 1448 by Donal McCarthy, Chieftain of Desmond, for the Observantine Franciscans, it was good to see that its ruin is still cared for and looked after. While walking over the Abbey my mind wandered back over time to the men who built this monument and cared for it for so long. The stone for this building came out of the ground, was shaped and put together to form the structure and many like it, and remained part of the land from which it came. Stark contrast from those built by modern man with his ability to process and destroy the natural beauty of the landscape and anything else in the way of progress.

Peter, an eleven-year-old who loves water and swimming; on sight of the water, wanted to strip off and jump straight into the lake. Wherever our travels took us, he would have his trunks with him. Much to his disgust, swimming was not allowed in these lakes, although we did manage to find a quiet spot to sit down and have a sly paddle in a shallow part of the lake.

Muckross House in the National Park was a sight to be seen. Its gardens were a feast to anyone who loves nature and the house is a good example of how the very wealthy lived. It was built in 1843 and is now administered by the National Parks and Monuments Service. There were examples of the trades carried out in the days of old, from saddle making to a blacksmith's shop. Many were still carried out, and craftsman could be seen at work.

Also in the house was a fine exhibition of local government in Kerry, during the Nineteenth Century, together with different types of housing from 1812 to 1971. The local History Society had done a good job in presenting this exhibition. By the time we rode back to Killarney to return our bikes and pick up my old Toledo, we had all we wanted from this very enjoyable trip. The following day we had high hopes of kissing the Blarney Stone, so off we went on our journey from Ballydaly up to Millstreet, then out on the open road to Macroom, continuing to Coachford, and the last lap, Blarney Castle.

The beauty that unfolded before us made my eyes moist as I drank in the power and strength of this wonderful land. The month of June and West Cork go well together. Most of the trees and fields were in full bloom and the little showers of rain we ran into seemed to have a smile on their faces, as though Mother Nature was playing games on us. The small villages we passed through had a magic of their own. In places like Carriganinny, Dripsey and Inishcacarra, imagination could take over so that if Judy Garland was to step out onto the road with her dog and strange characters from the film *The Wizard of Oz*, it would hardly have been surprising. The new bungalows and old cottages that were on banks up from the road, blended so much into the background that they looked for all the world like large plants with many different colours.

The road to Coachford was so natural, twisting, dipping and turning every hundred yards and, with all the wonder of nature to be seen everywhere, so unlike the flat, monotonous and drab roads that often run through cities. Without any warning on the right and spread out before us, was the River Lee coming down from the Sheehy Mountains. The road followed the twists and turns of the river for many miles. If there is such a thing as Paradise, then surely this journey would be a part of it. The river was so wide in parts that at first we thought it was a series of lakes.

We stopped a couple of times to inhale the soft breeze and fresh air. The narrow bank that ran from the roadside where we stood was covered in a pale green grass that gently made its way down to the water's edge. On the opposite shore, rising from the water, were many fields covered with trees and vegetation in different shades of green. Each time we stopped we had trouble restraining Peter from stripping off and plunging into the river!

Eventually we arrived at Blarney Castle. This had the kids excited and I felt a bit that way myself. After paying our entrance fee, we found ourselves in the grounds of the castle. It was tempting not to go into the fairy glade first so up we went, climbing the 100 stone steps. Any age group, young or old could, by taking their time, reach it. The younger ones were a little bit more adventurous in their haste to do so.

We reached the top and there it was, the Blarney Stone, the fairy tale come true. No longer did we have to think about it, or wonder if this object had come from the fertile mind of some Irish storyteller in days gone by. There, ready to be kissed by all those who had the nerve to lie on their backs looking for all the world as though they were waiting for `Madame Guillotine' with their head down, face pushed forward, ready to kiss that Emerald of the Emerald Isles, the Blarney Stone. Those who succeeded in kissing the stone were then deemed to be sent forth with the 'Gift of Eloquence,' which the stone bestows. Well that's what the legend says and surely it must be true?

THE STRANGER

In Liverpool City Centre, there are many fine buildings, and deep in the base of one of them was a group of tradesmen doing maintenance work. Their job was to carry out various works on the many services that ran through the subterranean passages of the building. During break times the men would make their way to the boiler house to have a cup of tea and a sandwich away from the prying eyes of the officials who worked on the upper floors in the Law Courts.

The three men had worked together in the passages of the building for many years. Bobby Maguire always had more to say than the other two and he worked out all the problems that they encountered. Bobby was the expert, whether right or wrong. Mick Manning was the joker who would always have a funny tale to tell. Then there was Johnny Nelson, who was the quietest of the three, always looking to Bob for the right answers, and to Mick for the laughter.

Bobby would always be first in the boiler house when it was time for the morning break. He would get there a couple of minutes before his two comrades to put the kettle on. As he entered on this particular morning a young man of about twenty-five was sitting on his favourite part of the bench. He was good-looking with a nice head of dark hair that had a blue sheen where the rays from the light bulb struck the crown of his head. His face was round with blue eyes, and he was not unlike Bobby, but much younger.

Bobby wanted to speak to him, but decided against it until Mick and Johnny arrived. 'Who was this cowboy?' he thought, as the young man sat in silence. All strangers were cowboys to Bobby. Mick was the next one to arrive in the boiler house. He looked first at the stranger and then cast his eyes in Bobby's direction.

"Who is this man, Bob, is he a new worker sent to give us a hand, or has he come to cadge a cuppa?"

"I don't know," was the reply, "you had better ask him yerself."

"Have they sent you down to give us a hand?" said Mick in a sarcastic manner, as he sat down next to the stranger. Johnny by this time had come into the boiler house and was seated waiting for Bobby to pour the tea but he could not take his eyes off the stranger. Being the quiet type, Johnny was not a man of many words but he felt drawn to speak to the young man.

"What are you doin' here lad, have you got a job to do?"

"No, I was just passing so I thought I would come in and sit down," said the stranger.

"What do you mean, you was just passing, we're right down in the bowels of the building, and you were just passing?"

"I didn't mean I was passing the building, I was down here and saw the light in your little boiler house, so I came in and sat down."

Mick was next to put a question to the young man.

"You're not from around these parts are ya? I thought there was something different about you."

Johnny was still sitting and staring at the stranger. He was sure that Bob and Mick would get to the bottom of it.

"Do you take sugar in your tea lad" asked Bobby "Thanks but I don't drink tea," was the answer.

"I've never seen you down here before." said Johnny, his eyes still fixed on the stranger.

"Well, I did work down here in the past."

"When was that?" asked Mick with a frown on his face.

"It was many years ago," was the reply.

Looking at Bob, Mick raised a finger to the side of his temple, as if to indicate that the young stranger was a little confused or retarded.

"How could you have worked down here many years ago," queried Johnny. "We would know if you worked in this building, we have been here a long time. You're much younger than us and we're in our late forties."

By now everyone was seated and ploughing through their sandwiches, leaving the young man to look on. It was at break times that the men would focus on the great social problems of the world, as, when their stomachs were satisfied, they could nourish and expound their own prejudices. Men have been deliberating important issues for years, but these three could, within minutes, dissect a carcass and fill it with their own prejudices creating in the process great confusion in their own minds.

"Bob," said Johnny, "you know in Russia male ballet dancers learn to box to stop them from getting female tendencies because of the movement of the dance."

"No, you've got it all wrong," said Bob. "That is not the reason they teach them to box. It's like this. In China they split the men from the women and put them all in separate communes, and that's what makes them gay. It's the same in Russia," continued Bob.

"I see," said Johnny, with a puzzled look on his face, but not daring to challenge Bob's brilliant analysis.

Mick was looking at the young man.

"I suppose you know your way around this building," he asked in a snide manner.

Johnny and Bob looked on and leaned over the table with their faces pushed towards the young man. The three characters waited for an answer to the question with expressions on their faces like schoolboys waiting for an explanation in the classroom.

"Yes, I do know my way around this building," said the young man.

"You must have worked the night shift, after we had gone home," said Johnny, with a satisfied grin on his face, believing he had made a well thought out statement. He looked in the direction of his two comrades for approval.

"Well you know, I suppose you could say I have been on the night shift," said the young man.

Johnny's confidence was increasing with each minute as he continued to interrogate the stranger.

"When did they let you out?"

"What do you mean when did they let me out?"

"Well, put it this way, lad. You come in here and sit down, then you tell us you've worked on this building and now you say you've worked on the night shift. We don't work night shifts here."

"I know you don't," he remarked.

"You're a bit strange aren't you?"

"Why am I strange, is it because you and your friends don't listen to what other people have to say?"

"It's not just that you're strange, it's because we don't take easily to strangers down here," said Mick.

"I can assure you that I am no stranger to this place," was the reply.

"Prove it," demanded Bob.

"Are you sure that you want me to do so?"

"If you can't, don't bother to come down here again," said Mick. He then looked at Johnny and Bob to make sure that they approved of his straight talk.

"Alright," said the young man. "I am what you would call a ghost."

Despite all their big talk, they became confused when confronted by anyone who had a clear cut and sober appearance, but now any respect that the three characters had for the young man with his smart appearance and his clear command of the English language and a demure manner, had gone.

"A ghost is it, well then let's see you walk through the wall," said Johnny.

"Yes, and how about putting your head under your arm," added Mick.

Now it was the turn of Bob, the thinker.

"Listen lad, have they let you out for the day, or have they brought you to the Law Courts because you've been scaring them in the nut-house?"

"Why have you become so angry towards me just because I told you that I am a ghost? You always dismiss anything that you don't understand so that things that you have a little knowledge of become distorted. In your mistaken belief that you have an understanding of the importance of your knowledge in your world, you only achieve confusion in yourselves, which you pass on to each other. If only you could stop and try to think about what you are actually saying, you would be far better off if you were prepared to listen to others sometimes. I have observed you for many years. You are good craftsmen, but you are immersed in your own petty little worlds."

The barrage of criticism from the stranger stunned Bobby, Johnny and Mick, who slopped tea down the front of his overalls. Bobby regained his composure and continued to look at the young man.

"You say you have been here a long time, so tell us about yourself before you go, and make it quick, because we're going back to work in a minute."

"I was a Civil Engineer, working on this building when it was being built and I slipped and fell down a deep shaft and was killed, my body was never found."

"Do you think we're as daft as you?" queried Bob.

Mick and Johnny were slapping their hands on the table and jumping up and down like idiots and making uncomplimentary remarks towards the stranger.

Bob, with his eyes still fixed on the young man retorted, "Right then, show us this shaft before you go, but I can tell you now, there is no shaft down here. If there was one I would know about it."

The young man led the way down subterranean passages, passing under the arches and arriving in an area that they had never been to before. There were no lights and the three comrades felt cold, more out of fear than anything else. They had stopped joking and kept looking at their young guide, who they now felt a lot more respect for and their scornful attitude had also disappeared,

"This, my friends, is where I fell and died."

In front of them was a narrow shaft, not much wider than the average man. Even though there were no lights in this area, they could see into the shaft; it looked so deep and bottomless. The three men were very quiet. Without commenting they gazed at their guide who was smiling now, as he had gained superiority. Being the boldest one, Johnny asked the stranger if they could go back.

"Certainly, I will guide you back."

The three of them walked behind the young man. The coldness of their unfamiliar environment slowly disappeared, and the lights of the passages once more came into view. They were really glad to see the lights ahead of them, and also thankful when they were seated back in their little boiler house. They remained silent as they sat motionless. Deep in their own thoughts, they could still feel the coldness of the dark passages clinging to their bodies. The scene in the boiler house was of three very dejected clowns, on a wooden bench in the middle of a circus ring. Mick the joker looking downcast, remained quiet. Bobby sat next to Mick, his head tilted to one side, his round face without expression, the mouth of his strong jaw hung loose, his heavy muscular shoulders leaned forward, supported by the strength of his arms firmly on his knees. Johnny, the silent and sensitive clown was sitting with his elbows on the table, his head pushed back, his face lifted towards the ceiling, and his blue eyes like empty pools without depth or reflection coming from them. The fair hair on his head hung like yellow strands of weeds from the overgrown gutters on an old derelict house. The comrades continued to sit, their bodies still motionless, their faces still blank, but in their minds they kept thinking about the young stranger, who had come amongst them. The young man had gone but things would never be quite the same in the subterranean passages.

They knew that they would never again find the dark cold passage or the young man who had been their guide.

THE MOURNERS

We were all seated on hard-backed chairs, pushed against the wall in the front parlour of an old Victorian house. All the available space around the walls had a chair, and a mourner occupied each chair. A large oak sideboard with triple framed mirrors was against one wall with two chairs ether side of it. The floral patterned wallpaper was turning to a sickly yellow colour in the places where it came into contact with the rays of sun that had managed to penetrate the curtains in the bay window.

Most of mourners sat in silence and looked down at the floor. Others looked nervous as they tried, without much success, to find a comfortable resting place for their posteriors on the wooden chairs. They were gathered because of the sudden death of Tommy Murphy and most in the room were still in a state of shock from learning of his death.

No one expected him to take his leave so soon, I mean to say, he was only fifty-nine years old, and to those getting on in years he was still a young man. To those who were younger, he still did not seem to be that old, but he was going to be missed by old and young alike. Tommy's landlady had provided the room for the mourners. She was a good soul who had looked after Tommy since his divorce after only two years of marriage. She was like a second mother to him, putting up with his moods of depression each time his money ran out and his trouser pockets were empty. Most of what Tommy earned would be handed over the bar counter at his local hostelry. He would buy friend or stranger whatever alcoholic refreshment they were fancied to.

Most of the mourners; friends, distant relatives, and

close relations, were unknown to one another. Some had attended out of respect and some to save face. Tommy would have introduced all of them had he still been in a position to do so, but being laid out in the local Chapel of Rest made that task impossible, even for him.

Standing on the doorstep of the terraced house were two of Tommy's friends. It was their job to keep a look out for the hearse making its way to the house from the Chapel of Rest. One of the men, a tall thin fellow with reddish cheeks and a nose to match, was wearing a dark suit that had seen better days and was not made for his height. He had his hands in his trouser pockets, trying to push his trouser legs downwards in the hope that they would make contact with the top of his shoes.

The second man stood to the side of the doorway with his back to the wall, a short stocky man smoking a cheroot. Every time he had a drag at the cigar, the smoke covered his pale round face. His belly protruded over the top of his dark grey trousers, which had been bought especially to enable him to create a good impression at the funeral. His dark leather jacket gave him an air of authority and every time he pulled his belly in he took another drag at his cheroot.

Back inside the house, an elderly aunt of Tommy's was quietly sitting by the oak sideboard and thinking about the Mass Card that she had for her nephew, in the vain hope it might assist in speeding his ascent into heaven. It would have been nice, she thought, if he could have been laid in an open coffin in the empty space in the middle of the room with everybody sitting around paying last respects. She then wondered if he would ever get to heaven, having been a terrible drinker and womanizer. She was glad his mother was not here at such a sad time, as she would not have been very happy knowing that Tommy would not be going to a plot in the cemetery to rest along side her and his father.

"God have mercy on them," the elderly aunt muttered to herself. "Poor Tommy will just be a tin of ashes leaving the crematorium."

Tommy liked his beer but then life had offered him precious little else, he was a kind and humble man who asked little from life, and little is what he got. That was what Tommy would tell his friends during one of his blue moods, but he had the sort of personality that had won him many friends. God gave him a six-foot frame, blue eyes and a stammer.

Any money Tommy earned from his labours as a merchant seaman, soon slipped through his fingers. Money was not for saving. It was meant to give pleasure, and most of his fulfilment came from standing in the bar of his local pub declaring Murphy's back in town. He would bang his two fists on the bar, then like the town crier, informing every one of the assembled drinkers, whether they be friend or foe, that the drinks were on him. The merrymaking would go on all day and night until closing time. The following morning Tommy would be lucky to have the price of a pint in his pockets. This happened when the chips were down and he would hope that one of his many friends would rescue him from the depths of despair by their generosity. He would often be seen standing outside his favourite watering hole when the linings of his pockets were like deflated balloons. Now that he had gone, his friends had come to pay their last respects and give him a good send off, but not only that, they had also made the arrangements for his funeral. If Tommy had been able to utter a few words at this time he would have said, "It is at times like this that you get to know who your true friends are."

Tommy had made many friends, far more than even he realized. God gave him a stammer but he also gave him the ability to communicate with his personality and sense of fairness. He was the sort of man who would take a hungry stray dog home to feed it. In the last few months at sea he had started to save some of the money that he had earned from his labours, the money was to be used for the only holiday he would have had in his life, but it was not to be, for fate had already mapped out the final chapter in his life. However before his sudden departure he had given instructions that the small amount in his post office savings book should be used to celebrate his life.

The tall man in the uncomfortable suit turned and poked his head into the lobby.

"They're here, they're on the way down the road." His voice gaining a higher pitch, "I see the hearse."

The mourners inside started to move into the lobby led by Tommy's elderly aunt.

"He was a good man, never did anybody any harm," she kept muttering to herself.

Still at the front door, the man in the leather jacket, the last of the cheroot between his fingers, was herding the mourners to the two funeral cars behind the hearse.

The elderly aunt climbed into the car, then turned to the woman behind her, saying, "You know, I shouldn't be in the first car, I hardly ever saw poor Tommy."

The woman just smiled the way people do at a funeral and guided the old lady into the car.

The hearse pulled away from the house followed by the mourners' cars, and in close pursuit about ten private cars carrying Tommy's friends from his local hostelry. A lone piper was waiting to lead the coffin into the Church, followed by the relations who only turned up when there was a funeral. The people inside filled every pew and throughout the Church and into the street could be heard the strains of *The Lark in The Clear Air*. Then the pipes fell silent for the mass to begin.

The Priest spoke of the man as if he had known him all his life. He talked about the dear departed soul who left no great wealth, works of art, or any other material possessions; yet he could attract so many people at his parting. After the Church service the mourners climbed into the cars and off they went to the crematorium much to the disgust of his aunt.

"If only his mother was here she would never have let him be cremated," she cried.

The piper fell silent after the last lament.

"He still have could have been with us if only he had been a good boy," cried Tommy's aunt as she climbed into the car for the ride back to the house with the mourners, where curly sandwiches and endless cups of tea awaited them. Most of Tommy's friends headed for the local pub to carry out Tommy's last wish, to celebrate his leaving. The beer flowed and the laughter rose, no mood of remorse could be felt. The thoughts and the talk were of Tommy and other old friends who had passed on. Someone remarked after nine, or was it ten pints, that he was sure that he could hear the sound of two fists pounding the bar and bellowing, "Murphy's back in town."

THE RED VELVET DRESS

She stood on the banks of the winding river.
Her long red velvet dress touched every
Contour of her body, as it flowed down to her ankles.

I looked entranced at the vision before me,
Her eyes did not catch mine.
The tall goddess figure, her large oval blue
Eyes, saw only the beauty of the winding river.

The waters pale blue and green, painted by a
Mixture of sunlight and clear blue sky.
The simmering sound of the waters, called
Out in perfect harmony.

The sun seemed to gather speed, as it
Descended into the west.
A vale of dark velvet, floated across the
Fading light, streaks of silver and gold
Flickering in the twilight.

The soft breeze floated across the dark green
Waters crashing against the river banks,
Rejoicing in the beauty of the winding river,
As it raced down to the sea.

Filled with enthusiastic delight my gaze was
Upon her and a smile from the tall vision of
Beauty in the long velvet dress was all that I
Longed for on the banks of the winding river.

MY NEIGHBOUR LEO

When I first met Leo I never thought for one minute that there would come a time when I would buy the house that had been his home for more than fifty years. Leo Farrell had been a near neighbour and he was getting on in years, being well into his eighties. He was a big man, over six feet tall, with a good head of lightish grey hair. He also had very good dress sense and was conservative in his appearance. He hailed from County Cork but I never found out exactly what part he was from. He could well have been from the same area as my own family in Cobh, a great seafaring town, but somehow we never seemed to get round to discussing it. Leo was a popular man amongst his neighbours. He could be described as a gentleman in both appearance and manner, someone who bothered few people. Leo's health was not too good in his advancing years but well-meaning folk, suggesting that he had help from Social Services, would be met with a look of disdain and a positive shake of his head.

There was only one other person who was allowed to be close to him and that was his next-door neighbour. She invited him in for Sunday dinner every week, when he would spend a couple of hours talking to her husband, an ex-ship's master. They had plenty in common, Leo having been a ship's radio officer all his working days, and when he finished at sea, Marconi Marine continued to employ him on land.

The large photograph of Leo at a company reunion dinner had pride of place in my home, formally Leo's. It was taken in 1946, depicting many Marconi people, sitting at tables with Leo nearest to the camera. The photo is now in the safe keeping of Liverpool's Maritime Museum.

His house was a large Victorian terrace house, with six steps leading up to the front door, and even had the row of bells hanging from a wall in the kitchen, so that the servants knew in which room they were needed.

Many effects belonging to Leo were found in the house, items that he had discarded, such as the large photograph of his working colleagues. Whenever you set foot inside you felt it had his stamp on it, as though he was letting you know that he had been around and was leaving his mark, like the young man carving his name on the bark of the tree. None of the rooms had electrical sockets for items such as an electric kettle or radio, but nevertheless you could see Leo's electrical genius as he would boil his kettle from the light socket and his radio could also be plugged into the same adaptor.

In the basement of the house could be found many parts of Marconi-type old radios and all the bits and pieces that once formed a radio network. One of the many things that Leo left in the house was an old microphone. He used to tell friends that King George V had used it, when he came to the City of Liverpool to open the new Mersey Tunnel linking Birkenhead with Liverpool. Leo had the job of installing the public address system that day in 1934, so it was his proud boast that the one he had in his possession was the very mouthpiece the King spoke into on that momentous occasion.

Perhaps Leo's brush with Royalty is tied up with his own ancestry, maybe a Ard-Ri ('High King of Ireland'), for it was in his early days as a sea-going wireless operator that he was given the post of 'Number One Wireless Operator' on the Royal Yacht. Alas, it was not to be, for he went down with appendicitis the very day he was supposed to embark. The Royal Yacht was not the only ship that sailed the seven seas, and when he recovered he was soon doing the job he loved. Ahead lay many adventures, which could be borne out by the hundreds of postcards from the many friends he had made over the years.

Everything Leo possessed had to be in its proper place, with postcards from all over the world, and letters, marked with the date he received them. Leo left so many things in this house, the house I was so lucky to buy. He left like a man walking out into the darkness, shedding his clothes, not wanting to look back. In a way Leo's possessions were his family, all of the items that would remind him of the sea and his days with Marconi, when it was good to be of some use to society, to have a skill that kept him in demand. Leo had never married, so had no sons, daughters or loving wife to greet him each time he landed on the shores of Liverpool, but he had many friends of both sexes and he still kept in contact with Ireland. Even the 'Cork Examiner' was sent to him from there, enabling him to keep in contact with County Cork, despite the many years away from his first home.

Leo was an orphan and that was as much as we could find out about this very private man. It is many years since he departed this world, although his presence still seems to remain in the home so many years later. After the sale of the house was completed, Leo was invited to stay on by the new owner, and certain refinements were added such as hot water. Previously this had come from a gas geyser in the kitchen, but the lead pipes were so silted up that very little water passed through them and the low pressure from the pipes stopped it from working. Electric socket points were also added to give further comfort and all the things that younger people take for granted, but were a luxury for Leo.

The day before the legal sale of the house was completed, Leo was taken into hospital. The house was due for a new face-lift with Leo's rooms taking priority.

Word came back from the hospital that Leo was doing fine and would be home soon, but this changed. Leo seemed to convey to those who visited him that he had had all he wanted from life. Being the gentleman he was he just fell a sleep the day after his eighty-seventh birthday, never to wake again. Life had nothing more to offer him.

THE GOOD NEIGHBOUR

It was a quiet, uneventful day. The only movement outside the small terraced house was the grey mist that rolled up the River Mersey on its journey from the Irish Sea. Seagulls and pigeons had gone to rest; even the sparrows clustered in little groups under the eaves of the roof. An overcoat of greyness was sweeping over the banks of the Mersey; it was Mother Nature's way of putting all life on the back burner. Most of the trees had shed their leaves, and the plants that lay around in the soil looked limp and tired. Had the window been open, the grey misty overcoat would have made its way into the warm, cosy room, but Billy had made sure that the window was securely closed to keep out the damp on this November day.

Billy was content as he looked out of the window. And why shouldn't he be? He had earned his retirement from the building trade. He looked pleased with himself as he sat in his easy chair, his broad hands going through the movements of lighting his pipe; they were still tanned, just like his round, weather-beaten face.

A soft breeze gently touched the water of the River Mersey during the summer months. The salt air and warm rays had given Billy's body the insulation it needed to get him through the first winter of his retirement. He puffed away, the smoke from his pipe covering most of his face, but this could not hide the pale blue eyes that shone through the haze.

Billy looked up from his pipe, and again cast a look towards the window. He could see that the mist had left damp streaks on the outer side of the glass. His blue eyes shone like beacons, smilingly, as he as gazed towards the cosy gas fire. He could see that one of the three radiants on the fire was broken. 'I had better be doing something to mend that, he thought. Mary, his friend and neighbour, had been at him for some time to get the fire fixed.

"Speak of the devil," he said to himself, hearing the key being pushed into the front door lock of his house. "That will be the little lady herself."

Billy's friend never ever knocked. She had the key to the house in order to take care of things whenever he was working away. Since his wife had died some years ago, Billy had lived alone. His children had married and moved away.

"I see you've done nothing about that damn fire," said Mary. "Instead of sitting on your arse smoking that pipe, you'd be doing yourself a favour if you stripped that fire down and got it working properly. And while you're at it, get into town and change the broken radiant."

"Aye," said Billy, with a tone that sounded like a man who had been caught shirking his work. "Mary," he continued, with a little meekness in his voice, "do you mind putting the kettle on, and we'll have a cup of tea, and then, I promise you, I'll get stuck into the job."

"You might be retired," Mary answered, "but you haven't lost the use of your arms and legs yet. Put it on yourself, I'm not your servant, nor your home help."

So reluctantly he made tea and they both sat drinking it whilst staring into the fire. Once again, Billy stoked up his pipe and struck four matches before he got the thing to light. Savouring the taste of his Erinmore tobacco, the scene was set for him to slip back into the tranquillity he had enjoyed before Mary had disturbed his solitude.

"Come on, for God's sake, do something with that fire. Those fumes are liable to lay you low forever."

Billy swore, but set to work dismantling the fire from its secure position in the hearth.

"Why don't you take the three radiants out first?" Mary added, "or it will not be just one you'll have to renew, it'll be all three of 'em."

"Stop your nagging," growled Billy. "Why don't you leave me alone to get on with the job? Can't you see the damn fire's heavy and I have to wrestle with it? I can do without you going on, but if it satisfies you, I'll take them out."

Billy threw the broken radiant into the waste bin, which stood at the left of the hearth and placed the other two on the floor.

"If you leave them sitting there on the floor, they'll get trodden on by those clumsy feet of yours," said Mary.

"Will you shut up, woman," said Billy, his voice rising in tone. "Before you walked in, I was enjoying the peace of me surroundings and me baccy on this, the first day of me retirement. You mean well, woman, but sometimes you sound like a bloody nagging wife."

"If you don't get your head together man, yer retirement will be a short one," was the reply.

"Don't be bothering me, the fire's out, and the job's being done, anyway."

Billy heard a loud knock on his front door.

"Go and see who that is hammering away. I hope to God it's not another one like yourself."

It was Tom, an old friend of Billy's who had come along to see how he was enjoying his first day off work.

"Come in and sit down," said Mary, "as you can see, Billy's busy."

"You seem to be enjoying yourself. What are you doin' with the fire?" asked Tom.

With a sarcastic tone Billy turned to his friend.

"Well now, Tom, I've decided to turn the fire round, so that the heat from it goes up the chimney stack. I thought it would be a nice change to be able to look at the back of the fire."

Mary giggled, and Tom shook his head as Billy laboured at his task.

"Will the two of you clear off while I get myself ready for town," Billy demanded.

Some hours later, Billy was back, kneeling on the hearth re-assembling the gas fire, and in walked Mary.

"Oh, I see you've nearly got the fire fixed back in position?"

"Yes, Mary, you're quite right, I've nearly finished. Since you came here this morning giving yer orders, I've had the time of me life. First I remove the monster from the hearth, almost rupturing meself in the process. Then, I placed the two good radiants on the floor, as instructed by yerself. While I was cleaning the chimney flue, the damned fire fell over, breaking one of the two good radiants that remained, leaving me with only one. So off I goes into town in the old banger, with the one and only precious radiant that I had left, on the passenger seat next to me. Coming up to the traffic lights I braked and the radiant slid slowly to the edge of the seat, toppled off and shattered into bloody pieces. Me first thought after that was to return immediately and strangle yerself. If I live to be ninety, I will always remember how you went out of yer way to make sure that I was kept very active on this, the first day of me retirement. It's not every man that is blessed with such a good friend and neighbour as yerself."

"Never mind the sarcasm, perhaps if you listen to me in future you will live to be ninety," answered Mary, as she put a light to the gas of the newly assembled radiants, pleased with herself that she had won the battle, and went off to reward him with another cuppa.

THE PRIZE FIGHTERS

Tom was sitting on the long bench with his back to the wall. He liked to sit in the same spot every night as it gave him a chance to see what was going on at the bar in his local hostelry. Sitting with him were his two friends, Mattie and Danny.

Danny was a man of sixty-seven years, and stood about five feet eight inches high. He still retained a lot of the solid frame that was his trademark when he was a younger man, and the pull of the fight game and the boxing ring had been his life from an early age. In fact, Danny was only fourteen when he first stepped into the prize ring of a boxing booth, hoping to earn a few shillings for staying three rounds against a much older and experienced boxer. The passing years had not diminished Danny's passion for this sport, and those of his friends who sat around the table knew that the only thing that mattered to him, apart from his family, was his love of boxing.

Danny was feeling a little nostalgic, but this mood was interrupted when he caught sight of his right ankle, which had swollen up and was starting to look like a ripe peach. Mattie was quick to notice Danny's look of concern.

"You make sure you get to the doctor in the morning, Danny" he said in a commanding voice.

Tom, with a little smile on his well-worn face, nodded his approval, by dropping his head from the left and bringing it round to the right in a forty-five degree angle, as though this was his neck exercise when he was a young man. Unlike Danny, old Tom had taken a few too many punches in his younger days, and whenever anyone tried to engage Tom in conversation, he would merely smile and nod. Tom was four years older than Danny but smaller in height and stature. Any evidence of him being an old prize-fighter had left his body. He was much slower than his two friends, Mattie and Danny, but on a good day his eyes still had some of the sparkle of his youth.

Mattie continued to lecture Danny about his ankle.

"Now don't you forget Danny, make sure you get to the doctor in the morning, or else there will be trouble between you and me."

Mattie was always concerned about the welfare of his two friends and they usually took some action to eradicate their problems when Mattie laid the law down. Mattie's boxing exploits had done him no visible harm. Outside of the boxing ring he was a good electrician and was still working at his trade. He was a man of fifty-eight and always well groomed. Because he was such a smart dresser, his old comrades loved to tease him by asking if he had just been to a wedding or funeral whenever he'd put a little extra effort into his attire.

"People will always take notice of you if you're neat and tidy," he would tell his companions when they mocked him.

"I've had a good night in the Gym. It is filled with lads from eight year olds to young men of twenty so I've got some promising kids and will get a few champions out of them," Danny would tell his two companions.

The gymnasium had given Danny a fresh purpose in life after the death of his wife, as his children were either married, or had moved away and were leading their own lives.

"Danny, how do you feel about those doctors who want to ban boxing, on the grounds that it causes brain damage?" asked one of the customers sitting at the next table.

"Brain damage?" said a very indignant Danny. "They

don't know what they're talking about. Do I look punchy, and what about dapper Dandy?" pointing to Mattie. "No one could accuse him of having brain damage."

Danny paused as his gaze fell on old Tom, and he failed to make any comment about him.

"One hundred and forty fights from the age of fourteen to thirty-four, and I earned every penny," he continued. "The college boys think they know it all, but I tell you, when you are born in a gutter, you have to learn to use your hands, or your feet, and anything else you have to survive in that jungle out there. We don't all get the chance to use our brains in a college. It must be nice to be a medical man or a professor, spouting about brain damage. Some of the lads I went to school with never had a boxing glove on, but they had brain damage long before they were thirty. If you tried to talk to them about the arts, music, theatre or a good book, they would just sit and grin like nut cases. Their brains were slowly beaten to death from the day they were born, as poverty and a stagnant life damaged their brains. Most working class kids will not have their brains working properly because of the sheer hopelessness of their lives."

Danny went silent, hoping that his outburst had not sounded like a lecture to his friends in the bar.

"You're right," said Mattie and Tom also gave a smile of approval.

They knew Danny always liked the chance to defend his sport and his way of life. His lifestyle had given him a chance to see new horizons, and meet people from many different circles of life. Danny's quick brain had not only absorbed punishment, but it still had the capacity for knowledge.

Mattie was shaking his head with the thought of Danny in pain, as the latter started to rub his swollen ankle knowing that he could have visited his doctor a couple of days earlier. Danny caught Mattie's expression and was waiting for a gentle scolding from him, but Mattie remained silent.

Still thinking of the past, Danny decided to recount the time he had boxed on the same bill as the great Benny Lynch. His two friends had often heard the story, but they were patient and allowed him to proceed. Danny always recalled his younger days when he was feeling down.

"I have seen Benny Lynch knock a man out with one blow, and when Lynch became famous, he started to knock himself about with the booze. I have watched him get knocked from one side of the ring to the other for five or six rounds when he would be observing his opponent's footwork, together with the position of his hands, and the movement of his body from the waist up to his head, which was the way he would slip away from punches.

All this information was fed into his brain, and the battle-lines would be drawn-up like a game of chess. He would wait for his opponent to move into the right position, then Benny Lynch would become the master and would strike out, felling his opponent motionless. Some people may call that brute force, but that would be wrong; only a genius like Benny Lynch could do that. The same man could measure speed and movements with his eyes."

By the time Danny had finished his tale, old Tom had slipped away and was heading home to his lonely little bed-sit.

Mattie rose from his chair, making ready to depart.

"Good night, Danny, I'm off home to get some beauty sleep."

His old friend was too engrossed in the past to notice the departure of his two old comrades, so Danny was left with his memories.

The following night, Danny was missing from the bar.

"Good evening to you Tom," said Mattie, as he sat down next to his old friend.

Tom was in a happy frame of mind but his moods of silence had increased over the passing months, much to the despair of his two comrades.

"I can see by the look on your face that Danny will not be calling in tonight."

Tom gave Mattie a half smile and a slight nod of his head at Mattie's comment.

"It must be that leg of his."

"What's that you're saying, Tom?"

"I was thinking it must be his ankle still playing him up. Nothing else would keep him away, unless he has given up the ghost and somebody is laying him out this very minute, and making him ready for the shroud."

"Now that's a nice thing to be saying about your best friend, and him probably lying there in agony with that ankle of his."

"It's as well, that he is not here now listening to you," said Mattie, with a twinkle in his eyes as he turned his head to look straight into Tom's face.

A smile spread across Tom's face after realising he had amused Mattie, it had cast away some of the shadows that had engulfed it in the last few months. For a few seconds the smile allowed Mattie to see the face that he remembered in their younger days.

Mattie and Danny, more than most people, had noticed the change in Tom's mental and physical appearance. 'How the years had passed,' thought Mattie. It seemed like only yesterday when he had sat and watched Tom move around the boxing ring, like a young dance master throwing his opponent off balance before landing his punches with speed of a rapier.

"Mattie, are you still working at your trade?" asked Tom.

The question startled Mattie and brought him back from memory lane.

135

"Yes, yes, Tom, I'm still at the trade, but things are not looking too good at the moment with the depression, or lack of opportunity, as some people choose to call it. Anyway, Tom, you're in a very talkative mood tonight. I'm glad to see you're like this, it's a change from listening to Danny going on about the state of the world."

"Do you think he will be alright Mattie?"

"Do you mean Danny?"

"Yes of course I do, will he be alright?"

Mattie could see that his old friend was becoming agitated.

"If it makes you happy, I will call on him tonight, when I am making my way home."

Mattie's decision to take some positive action to make sure that Danny was not alone and suffering, seemed to please Tom. He smiled and stretched his two arms to allow his hands to cover his knees, and at the same time hunched his shoulders as though he was easing the pressure on his muscles. Tom was now content and oblivious to what was taking place around him. He did his stretching exercises, as he would do in his younger days, waiting for the bell to sound for the next round. While Mattie was concerned about Danny's health in recent weeks, he was becoming more disturbed with Tom's more frequent moods of silences and lapses of memory.

Unlike Danny, Mattie was not concerned for the rights or wrongs of the world. What mattered most to him were his friends and his trade as an electrician. It was only on rare occasions that Mattie could be drawn into any sort of reminiscence of his boxing exploits.

Although Mattie was the younger of the prize fighters, there was little that he did not know about his two friends, or they about him. Tom's father was a big man with a square head and very little brain. He would lecture Tom on the benefits of being able to defend himself, as any protests at not wanting to be a pugilist would be brushed to one side. Despite his background, Tom was bright and a very capable athlete, who mastered most sports. The very sport that Tom rebelled against in his young life was to be the one that he mastered above all others. Tom looked towards Mattie.

"What are you thinking about Mattie? You're sitting there very quiet."

"Oh, it's nothing very important. I was just thinking about the old days."

Tom seemed reassured and sat back in his seat, facing the bar to survey the scene in front of him: he had a lot of pleasure watching the coming and going of friends and strangers alike. When the bar was clear of customers for a few minutes, the staff would pass the time of day with Tom and his comrades. His favourite barmaid was a dark-haired, busty girl with big blue eyes, who would often give Tom a special little smile and a wink. Danny and Mattie would derive pleasure from watching Tom's face light up when this happened, for they knew that a smile from this pretty young girl would remind Tom of his youth. Not only did this pleasant girl have the same name as Tom's first girlfriend, when he was sixteen, but the resemblance was also striking.

Tom's two friends knew the sort of memories Elizabeth would evoke in him. She had started school on the same day as Tom and they lived only a few doors away from each other. Tom would recall to his two lifelong comrades how he would sometimes walk along the canal bank with Elizabeth. At times during the summer months this waterway could smell like a cess-pit as it made its way along the back of the hovels where they lived, winding its way to the docks and the river.

The Leeds Liverpool canal had been very much a playground for Tom and his friends. On a warm day most of them would swim naked, as even if you were lucky enough to own a pair of bathing trunks, it was not manly to wear them. Tommy's first encounter with the murky waters of the Leeds and Liverpool canal was a frightening experience. When he was nine years of age, he was taken by the hand and led to the water's edge by Slasher Smith, his father, who made him undress, exposing the frail body of his son.

After removing his own clothes, except for his battered trousers, he lifted Tom above his head and flung his young son into the middle of the stinking canal, as he would a dead cat. This crude method of teaching had been demonstrated in the past by Slasher Smith, when he had taught Tom's elder brothers in the same way. When his son's body hit the water, Slasher followed into the slimy water and proceeded to swim around him. Flailing his hands in the water, Tom attempted to keep himself afloat with Slasher shouting words of encouragement. Round and round his father would swim, like an old porpoise, pushing the young boy back to the surface every time he started to submerge. Tom was not allowed out of the water until he could swim. Like his elder brothers, he left the water eventually, knowing that when again he entered the murky canal water, there would be no fear of him drowning. He would be just as competent a swimmer as the rest of the neighbourhood kids.

Elizabeth's parents were very determined that their daughter would not continue her friendship with Tom. They were completely against their daughter having any sort of relationship with a boy who had taken up boxing as a sport. Her parents moved away from the district, and Tom never saw Elizabeth again, and throughout his youth and manhood, he never had a serious relationship with a woman.

"Well, I think I'll be off," said Tom, "I've had enough

for one night. It's been a bit miserable without Danny being here, don't you think so, Mattie?"

"Oh, I see, my company is not good enough for you" said Mattie, "Just because your old pal, Danny, is not here, you're off."

"Now it's not that I don't enjoy your company Mattie, but you know it's always nice to have Danny chatting here with us."

"Yes, I understand Tom, I've missed Danny just as much as you have tonight, but don't worry about it old friend, I'm sure he will come hobbling through that door tomorrow night."

"I hope so," replied Tom.

"Do you mind if I walk back with you to your place, and you can make me a nice cup of coffee before I go my way home?" asked Mattie.

Entering Tom's bedsit, Mattie saw many mementoes of Tom's boxing exploits. Hanging on the wall were a number of photographs, one being of the only woman that Tom had been devoted to; his Mother. She had been small and gentle with great humility, despite being married to someone as aggressive as Slasher Smith. It was her gentle qualities and appearance that Tom had inherited. Apart from the large number of trophies that Tom had won in his amateur days, this tiny bedsit was very sparsely furnished.

In one corner of the room was a small single divan bed and by its side, a straight-backed wooden chair where Tom kept his pyjamas and, under which were his slippers. Facing the bed, in the far corner, was a three-quarter size wardrobe, which had seen better days, and next to it, stood a small cupboard with two drawers. The top of this cupboard was littered with more of Tom's trophies and many of them looked as though they had seen better days; some must have been fifty years old.

Mattie sat in an easy chair, alongside a drop-leaf table, while Tom prepared their coffee in a small recess, which served as a kitchen. The bed-sit was clean and bright. He watched Tom's movements as he was preparing their nightcap. 'If there is such a thing as God,' thought Mattie, Then why does he allow someone as gentle as Tom to end his life in this lonely way.'

Mattie and Danny had witnessed the deterioration of Tom's health over the past couple of years. As he watched his old friend perform the simple task of preparing a cup of coffee, he wondered how long it would be before Tom could not distinguish between making a cup of coffee, or a cup of tea.

"It was good to see you in such a talkative mood tonight Tom, you haven't gone and got yourself a little woman have you, and are keeping her to yourself?"

"Of course not, Mattie. I'm off them for Lent."

"Away with you man, a little lady friend would do you the world of good."

Mattie stretched his legs and slipped his hands into his trouser pockets. He pushed his head back onto the chair and looked into Tom's face, with a mischievous grin and waited for his reply.

"Me, have a woman? Do you remember the last one I had pushed onto me by Danny, trying to be a matchmaker? Do you remember Mattie? Yes, you remember alright, sitting there with a grin on your face."

Mattie was pleased at the way Tom confronted him and went on, "The one with the monkey? Remember it was when I had that horrible little flat, the one I had before I got this place. Danny said to me, 'will you let this poor woman stay with you for a few days. She's stranded in Liverpool and has nowhere to go. If you take her in, I will try and get her fixed up with some accommodation.' Yes, that's Danny; the Good Samaritan."

Mattie snorted with laughter.

"It was alright for you and Danny," Tom continued, "you didn't have to live in the same house as the silly cow. I don't know who was the worst, her or the monkey. Not only did I have to take the woman in, I had to suffer her monkey as a lodger as well. Yes, you can sit there grinning like a Cheshire cat but I was the one who had to suffer the silly woman for two weeks; that is until I rebelled."

Still with his legs stretched out in front of him and both hands in pockets, Mattie concentrated on Tom's movements and speech. He could see the smile building up on Tom's strong features. Although this woman had disturbed Tom's quiet existence, he could always see the funny side of his encounter with her.

"It's often said that animals grow to look like their owners," said Tom. "But, I tell you Mattie, that one was possessed by that monkey. She was a terrible sight when she went into a rage, walking around in her bare feet with her teeth in a glass on a chair by the side of her bed. The only time she wore her shoes was when she went out to buy food for herself and that monkey. I felt in mortal terror of the two of them. When the postman called, it would be first to the door moving like a blasted rocket."

"Who would be first to the door?" asked Mattie.

"The monkey of course. You know quite well what I mean."

The look of delight left Tom's face for a brief moment because he felt that he had been rudely interrupted by Mattie's nonsense.

"Where was I? Oh yes, the monkey. Well he would be at the door before I was out of my chair and yelling with pleasure as he picked up the mail the postman had pushed through the letterbox."

"I wish I'd have had a monkey to collect my letters

from the front door," said Mattie.

"Will you stop interrupting me and let me get on with it. The next thing, it would be sitting on my armchair, opening the mail, much the way you and I would open a letter, then it would proceed to read the damn thing."

"Now Tom, who is trying to make a monkey out of who?" said Mattie.

Tom was becoming annoyed at Mattie's continued interruptions and this manifested itself by shakes of the head as Tom picked up his mug of coffee from the table as he was about to sit down. Mattie could see that he had upset Tom by his frivolous behaviour.

"I'm sorry, Tom. It's just that I find the whole idea of the monkey opening your letters so funny. I know that you are not telling me a tall story, so please accept my apologies Tom, there was no harm meant."

"I know you didn't Mattie. Anyway, drink your coffee, it's lying there going cold."

For the first time, Mattie saw the mug of coffee in front of him, realising then that he had become so immersed in Tom's description of the monkey that he had forgotten about it.

Sipping their nightcap, the two friends sat together in silence, apparently oblivious of each other's presence. Mattie broke the silence.

"Well, Tom, I will have to be leaving you. I've had a hard day today and I've got some heavy work ahead of me tomorrow."

Mattie lifted himself from the comfortable armchair and stretched his arms above his head, but there was no response from Tom as Mattie made ready to go. Tom sat with his coffee in his hand, and in silence gazed towards the floor.

"Tom, I will be off now."

There was no reply, apart from a nod of the head. As

Mattie opened the door to leave Tom alone in his little bedsit, Tom looked up from the floor.

"Oh, goodnight Mattie, God Bless, and may all your troubles be little ones."

Mattie smiled as he closed the door behind him.

BILLY'S PAWNSHOP

Billy's Pawnshop, never use it myself, but I know a
Few that do. Pawn my hat and coat, a thing I would
Never do, but I know a few that do.
Billy's Pawnshop, not the place for me.

To stand in line like others do, to pawn my clothes
And shoes, not the thing I would do, just to have a
Bob or two. Would much prefer to get my shopping
From the corner shop like others do.

On tick of course, or should I say on credit, the way
Nice people do, the pawnshop, I am afraid it's not
The place for me, pawn my ould man's boots, a
Thing I would never do.

Sooner starve than go to Billy's Pawnshop the way
Other people do, Missy Murphy's the paper shop,
Or should I say the newsagents, the way nice
People do, and her parrot, or was it a cockatoo.

It's cage hooked to the wall, outside the shop, on a
Fine day, he would shout to embarrass you, have
You been to the pawnshop too? Lets not forget
Charlie McCarthy, the coal man.

He would stop outside of Missy Murphy's with
His horse and cart, then the parrot, or was it a
Cockatoo, would shout to the horse have you
been to the pawnshop too.

You're a silly old parrot, or what ever you are, it
Would shout don't you know that a horse can't
Go to the pawnshop, but I know some people
That do, and it's not Charlie McCarthy.

Because Charlie's got more than a bob or two,
And those dockers, I've seen them go to Billy's
Pawnshop, pawning their hooks, just to get a bob
Or two to spend in the local hostelry

Not me, or my ould man, we would never go to
The pawnshop to get a bob or two, to spend on a
Pint or two, we are respectable people and if
Need be, we get credit the way nice people do.

MEMORIES OF AN EXILE

The little man was sitting on a wooden box, watching the passengers disembark from the boat, which had just arrived after a night-crossing from Dublin. Many seemed excited at the thought of seeing Liverpool for the first time. They seemed cheerful and had the feeling that they knew where they were going. The little old man looked at the happy people, and thought about the time he was a passenger landing in Liverpool after an awful night-crossing on the cattle boat. He was deep in thought, contemplating them as, well-dressed, they rushed off to all different destinations, which had already been arranged before they left. Whilst the old man sat watching and wondering, a smile spread over his face. A young man in his early twenties, and on his own, stood looking at him.

"Excuse me, sir," he said as he approached the elderly one, "do you live in Liverpool?"

The old man shook himself out of his thoughts, looked at the young man and replied, "Yes, I have lived in this town a long time and my name is Patrick."

"How long is that, sir?" said the young man.

Patrick did not answer but just sat and smiled at the young man.

"Then may I ask, sir, how old you are?"

"Yes, you may ask, I am three generations old."

"But how can that be sir?" queried the young man.

"It was because I was born in 1843 in a little house in Carrigaline in the county of Cork, and I travelled with my parents to Liverpool in 1847 and have been here ever since."

The young man looked at Patrick who was still sitting on the wooden box, and his gaze contained a sadness and compassion for the old man. Patrick looked straight into the eyes of the young man.

"No, I am not confused, I really am three generations old. I once stood where you are standing now, after stepping off the boat with my parents. I was four years old and I can still remember the bundles of old clothes they carried in their worn hands. When we moved away from the docks we had nowhere to live, as was the fate of many of us Irish who came to England at that time. Now, you are a well-fed young man with fine clothes and I wonder if you have ever given a thought to your fellow countrymen who were exiled in this town. Would you like to see where my family went to live, it is only a short distance from here?"

"Yes, I would," said the young man, knowing he still had plenty of time before he caught the London-bound train. As they walked together, he noticed the large warehouses that were busy stacking and stowing goods going to or from the ships. Queuing up outside the warehouses were many horse-drawn carts and wagons, waiting to unload or load their cargoes. The young man thought it was strange to see so many horses and wagons. The thought crossed his mind that it was now 1982 and even in Dublin itself there were no longer any such wagons. Then he noticed another young man around the same age as himself, standing in the doorway of a warehouse, dressed in unfamiliar clothes. In fact this person looked like a younger version of Patrick. He turned to him and said, "That man standing in the doorway there bears a strong resemblance to yourself. Is he a relative of yours?"

Patrick just looked at his companion with the same silent countenance as before and with the same smile that had induced the young man to approach the quaint little figure at the dockside. He asked Patrick if he would mind him speaking to the man in the warehouse doorway.

"It's impossible for you to do that," was the reply.

"But why?" said the younger man.

"Well, you're a stranger to that man and he would not relate to you."

"But I don't understand," said the young man.

"You will one day," was the answer, "when you are three generations old."

The young man looked at Patrick again with a look of compassion in his eyes. His frail friend led him on through the strange streets of Liverpool, and after a short time Patrick said, "This is where my family came to live when I was just four years old."

The young man found himself walking into a courtyard, but not the type that housed the landed gentry of the past. This one had little narrow houses on each side and a midden (a lavatory without water) at the far end, with a narrow passage to gain entrance to the yard. The houses were so narrow that they looked as if they had been pushed together by two huge fists. Altogether there were eight such buildings. In the middle of the courtyard was a standpipe with people drawing water from it. The young man asked Patrick why they were doing this.

"It is because they have no water in the houses and this pipe is their only means of obtaining water. It is only turned on for one hour twice a day," was the answer.

He also noticed that there were many folk standing outside the houses, and was about to ask the reason for this, when the old man looked at him.

"You have a long way to travel with me, through three generations and much to learn," he said. "These people live in houses with such tiny windows which let in little fresh air and when it does manage to come in, it is soon swallowed into the empty lungs of the many people who are crowded in the houses. That is why they stand outside when the weather is warm enough."

"I've noticed that many of the people have Irish accents. It's as if I was still back in Ireland."

"Young man, you have many things to learn. A chameleon may change its colour many times, but he will always remain a chameleon. Come with me now and I will show you where I lived when I was a young man." They continued, the young man walking alongside his companion. He noticed that the streets were not quite as strange or as dirty as when they were walking near the warehouses.

"This is where I used to lived," said Patrick, breaking the silence.

"Oh, I see," said the young man, "it is called Dublin Street."

"Right," said the other.

When they turned into the street, the young man could see two blocks of tenements with open landings and a stairway in the middle leading to each landing. Patrick kept looking at the young man as if expecting a change of expression to appear on his face. The latter turned to Patrick.

"Sir," he asked, "why is it I see people who resemble you so much?"

Patrick just smiled as the young man added, "Look up there on the second landing, I can see a middle-aged man who resembles you."

"You will understand soon," said Patrick, still smiling.

"You keep telling me that I will one day understand, but Sir, you can be no more than eighty-five years old, and yet you say that you were four years old in 1847. If that were so, you would be now a great age indeed."

"I see that you can think for yourself," said the old man with a mischievous little smile enlivening his withered face. Now his companion was more than a bit confused and said, "You say that you are three generations old, but as far as I am aware, a person can live but one life."

"That," replied the old man, "is because unlike the chameleon, you will forget what you are, and where you come from."

"But Sir, just like me, you are trapped inside one generation."

"No longer am I trapped, like the chameleon, I now remember quite clearly what I am, where I came from and, more importantly, why I came to a city lying on the opposite side of the Irish Sea."

The pair continued walking and a few yards further on Patrick stopped and turned.

"This is where I live now. Please go on into the flat. The door is open and I shall follow you in after I have had a quick word with my neighbour."

The young man entered, and after a little time in the flat he noticed three framed photographs placed on an old mahogany sideboard. Two of the three photographs were obviously taken many years ago and were faded but the third, which must have been taken recently, was of the old man. At that moment he turned to see a middle-aged lady standing in the doorway.

"Are you a relation of the old gentleman?" she asked.

"No, but we met a little earlier and he wanted to show me his home."

A puzzled expression came over her face.

"The old man you are talking about died just a few minutes ago in my flat and the last words he uttered were that he was three generations old."

The young man looked back at the photos and walked out of the flat and into the bright sunshine to be forever puzzled.

THE MIDWIFE

Maurice felt very relaxed and in a happy frame of mind as he walked through the village of Passage, Cobh, County Cork. He paused to look up at the sign over the little café. 'What a quaint name,' he thought to himself, 'The Tiny Tea Shop. Can this really be the place or have I got the address wrong? It must be here,' Maurice kept repeating to himself. 'Have I really arrived. Is this where my grandfather lived all those years ago?' The questions kept coming into his mind as he tried to keep them in order with his thoughts racing. His excitement was starting to make him feel a little nervous.

"Calm down, man," Maurice said aloud to himself, as he pushed the door open to the sound of the clang of an old-fashioned spring bell, "Jesus, it's enough to waken the dead." He saw the archaic device that warned the proprietor that someone had entered the establishment. Maurice looked around the brightly decorated room, the ceiling was painted white and the walls were pink. Hanging from the centre of the ceiling was a brass lamp. Maurice stretched himself to his full height and stood on his toes to look up at the lamp to see if it was powered by electric power or oil.

Four round tables with gingham covers filled most of the room. On the hearth stood a gas fire, where at one time an open fire would have been the focus of attention on a cold winter day. In the far corner of the room, sitting at one of the little tables, was an elderly lady who had lifted her head when she heard Maurice. Their eyes met and she gave him a friendly smile but she did not speak before she dropped her gaze again, giving the impression that she did not want to be disturbed by idle chatter.

Maurice was still standing and had not selected the table to sit at.

"Can I get you anything, Sir?"

Turning, Maurice saw a dark haired young man.

"Can I help you?"

"Oh, yes," said Maurice. "Could I have a pot of tea and a cheese sandwich, please?"

"Certainly, I'll not be more than a few minutes as my wife has just put the kettle on."

With a friendly smile the young man continued, "We don't have many customers first thing on a Monday morning."

"That's alright," replied Maurice, "there is no rush. I am on holiday, and have plenty of time. As a matter of fact I am looking up old names and addresses, with the hope of tracing some of my ancestors. My grandfather came from these parts and settled in Liverpool where I was born."

The young café owner showed a polite interest in Maurice's quest, having heard it so many times before from tourists visiting the town.

"It would appear from the information I have that my grandfather was born in this very house, at a time when it was just a family home," continued Maurice.

The young man appeared to be a little puzzled at Maurice's remarks.

"This sounds very interesting," he said, "I must tell my wife. I'll just give her your order."

Maurice sat down and watched the owner disappear into the back room. He wondered whether the man had thought him foolish, standing talking about his grandfather. 'Ah well, I suppose a middle-aged man talking about his ancestor to a stranger does sound a little foolish.'

He felt very content sitting in the small room that his grandfather would have sat in all those years ago. The café was one of a number of small terraced houses, probably more or less the same as it was when his grandfather had lived in it. He continued to absorb every detail of the room, thinking how nice it would be if he could look over the rest of the place, and how interesting it would be to walk around what had once been his ancestral family home.

"I knew your grandfather, Maurice," said the old lady sitting in the corner of the room.

Maurice was startled by the remark, for he had paid little attention to her when he entered the café, in case he was intruding on her privacy. He sat in disbelief, looking at the smiling woman.

"I am sorry if I upset you, but I did know him."

As if in a trance, Maurice continued looking at her.

"I suppose you think I am just a senile old woman? Well you would be quite wrong."

Maurice did not answer. For the first time he had a good look at the woman who had thrown his mind into confusion. She had dark hair despite her age and her hands were slim and her fingers long. He saw that she was wearing a dark navy-blue blouse, with a narrow collar and a row of very fine pearl buttons holding it together. A light grey shawl covered her shoulders and a long dark blue skirt fell loosely to her ankles, her feet were in leather lace-up boots. Maurice could not account for the strange feeling that he had as he looked at her strong facial features and light blue eyes.

'How could she know my name?' he was thinking. 'Perhaps I introduced myself when I spoke to the café owner, as I entered the café. Yes, that must have been it.' Not wanting to offend the old lady, Maurice addressed her in a gentle voice.

"How could you possibly know my grandfather? He would have left this house in the early part of the 1900s."

"Oh, but I did," was the reply. "You see Maurice, he left this house the year I departed your world. All my life I lived in this house, until I died in very tragic circumstances."

By now Maurice had forgotten his surroundings because his mind and thoughts were focused only on the woman.

"Would you like to tell me how you came to die in this house?"

Maurice was shaken by what she had said and a cold feeling seemed to run down his spine.

"Yes, I will tell you," came a quick and firm reply. "On the day I died, it had been a long and tiring one for me. I was the unofficial midwife, with two expectant mothers to attend to that day and I saw two lovely children come into the world. I retired to the room just above the one we are sitting in. We had no electricity or gas in those days, only paraffin lamps or the open fire. I made my way up the stairs with my paraffin lamp and placed it on a small table beside the bed close to the door of my room. Normally I would put the lamp into the middle of the table but giving no thought to what I was doing, I put it near the edge of the table; something I would not have done if I had not been exhausted. As I turned away from the table, I knocked the lamp with my arm and started a fire, with a sheet of flame shooting up the door and soon the room was engulfed in smoke. I could hear people outside, trying to get to me but the flames spread throughout the room within seconds, trapping me forever."

Maurice was sitting motionless when he felt a hand on his shoulder. The young man had returned with his order.

"Are you alright?" he said.

Maurice looked up and smiled at the café owner, but

the smile only conveyed a look of fear in his face. A tray had been placed on the table in front of him holding the tea and the sandwich he had ordered.

"You don't look too well," said the owner. "Here, let me pour you some tea."

Without waiting for a reply the young man started pouring from the pot as Maurice sat without protest.

"Drink it down, you will feel better."

"Thank you," answered Maurice as the man walked away. Maurice looked over to where the old lady was sitting, but she was no longer there – only an empty chair. The café owner had returned to the dining room with a fair-haired young woman, in her early thirties. It was clear for all to see that she was in the latter stages of pregnancy.

"My husband, Peter, has just been telling me about your grandfather. I would like to know more – it sounds fascinating."

The young woman showed a growing interest in Maurice as he related his story and suggested, "Would you like to come into the back room, it's more comfortable."

Without protest, Maurice followed the young woman.

"Sit yourself down and make yourself at home," said the young woman, pointing to a large easy chair. Maurice sat back but felt it would not be wise to get too comfortable otherwise he would fall asleep. Peter and his wife were kept busy in and out of the kitchen, and left Maurice to his thoughts as he went on thinking about his experience in the café. 'Did I imagine all that took place in the next room? If I tell this young couple about the old woman they would think I was having a breakdown. Must be my mind playing tricks on me. Yes, that's what it must be, my feeling of going back in time when I came into this café.'

Whenever there was a lull in their work, Peter and his wife joined Maurice in their living room.

"I don't suppose your name would be Sheils?" Maurice asked the young couple. "You see that was the name of my grandfather, Maurice Sheils, the same as myself."

"Is that so?" said Peter. "Our name is Sheils and of course you know my first name is Peter and my wife's is Mary."

The young woman smiled at Maurice before she spoke.

"Maurice, that is quite a coincidence, our name being the same. I was a little bit concerned for you. When I went back into the café earlier on, you seemed deep in thought, staring into the corner of the room. There was no one else in at the time, just yourself, and you were probably casting your mind back to how it might have been if your ancestors had not left this village. Will you stay for a while and tell us all about yourself and your grandparents?"

"Yes, I would love to stay a while," said Maurice, but he kept turning over in his mind what the old lady had said to him.

Mary seemed glad to sit and have someone to talk to as she was expecting her first child within the next day or so. A few years earlier, the young couple had bought the house and obtained planning permission to turn part of it into a café. They talked to Maurice long into the evening, despite the interruption of the odd customer. He enjoyed the company of the bright and friendly pair, and talked freely of his family history.

"Have you found anywhere to stay or will you spend the night with us? Our guest room is free," asked Mary. Before Maurice could answer, Mary continued, "You will be able to come and have a drink in the bar down the road later, with Peter and I."

"Right, you've talked me into it," was the reply.

The bar was a homely place and it was not long after they arrived that the main room became packed with people. He was the only stranger there, and his Liverpool accent was of interest to some of the other customers.

"Are you enjoying yourself, Maurice, sitting with all of us, and not another scouser in sight?" chuckled Mary, "but I must say you seem very much at home here."

"I'm always at home when I'm in Ireland, Mary, you see, it's still in my blood," answered Maurice.

Mary smiled and patted her stomach.

"Normally I would have been in bed by now; at the end of a day I am usually worn out, but it won't be long now, soon it will be all over."

Although Maurice was listening to Mary, he could not help looking towards Peter, who was speaking to a man who had just entered the bar. The latter was talking in a low voice and when he finished talking to him the man hastily left the bar. Peter returned to Mary.

"I won't be long, stay here with Maurice, I'll be back in a few minutes."

Mary knew by the sound of his voice that something was wrong. She turned to Maurice,

"Will you go and see if Peter is alright?"

Outside people were running up the road, so Maurice ran after them and found Peter standing outside the café in a state of shock. Smoke and flames poured from the upper rooms. The owner turned to Maurice.

"It's as well you came along today, because we would not have been out socialising, and my wife would have been in bed in that room."

Maurice could hear the voice of Peter as he extended his gratitude to him for turning up, but his eyes and thoughts were firmly fixed upon the window above the café. Although it was belching smoke and flames he felt certain he could see the figure of the old woman in the window. Later it was confirmed that nobody had perished in the fire, but Maurice could not put it out of his mind that he saw a woman who appeared to be dressed in Victorian clothes.

BLACK JACK'S

The Clyde Public House was only a stone's throw from the Liverpool docks and most of its clientele lived in the streets that surrounded it. The older people in the community always referred to it, as 'Black Jack's' and it was common knowledge that the first Manager was a big dark-haired man with a black beard who was always known as Black Jack. When the men in the community wanted to relax from a hard day's labour on the docks, Black Jack's was the place to be. Well, that was how it seemed to me when I was a young boy growing up just a few hundred yards from this establishment. It was when I reached my early teens that I took the trouble to read the large gold-painted letters, 'The Clyde Public House' above the frosted glass window, and realized its true name. Like most children I took more notice of the spoken word, so 'Black Jack's' became imprinted on my mind.

After discovering the correct name I decided to find out the true history of 'Black Jack's, so I decided to ask my Dad, thinking he would be the one to give me the right answers.

"Well, it's like this," he said. "Many years ago, the Manager was a big fella with a back as straight as a guardsman, and he was from County Kerry."

Although I nodded in agreement, I did not have any inkling of where or what County Kerry was.

"This man," my father continued, "had a head of hair as black as coal, just like your mother's, a black beard that seemed to cover most of his face, and although a gentle giant of a man, he was still a fearsome sight, especially if any one decided to disturb the peace in his establishment. He was always referred to as Black Jack, so that's how the name came about."

"Is he still in the pub?" I asked.

"No, he is long since gone and I imagine he will be up there with the angels," was the reply.

'Black Jack's' backed onto the Leeds and Liverpool Canal, which twisted and turned its way down to the River Mersey. Most of the lads in the area had their first swimming lessons in the canal down by the docks. I do not remember any of the girls in the area taking the plunge, but then who could blame them; they must have had more sense than to jump when it was often used as a common dumping ground. A dead dog or cat floating by never got in the way of our enjoyment, and, as we never had the luxury of going to the swimming baths with a towel, a pair of swimming trunks and the entrance fee, we had to leave it to Mother Nature to provide for us.

When the swimming session was over we would stand shivering on the bank with our hands crossed to save embarrassment while waiting to share the one towel between six or seven lads; that's if we were lucky enough to have one, of course. Many a drama was played out in that canal; most times they would be happy but on other occasions they could be sad, as the canal was no respecter of persons. 'Black Jack's' continued to offer liquid refreshments and the chance to relax from the rigours of life. I suppose to most people in this enlightened age it would seem like a strange hostelry, but it served its purpose. It was only a very small establishment and the bar was adorned by men only. Not that women were not allowed in it, but no self-respecting women would want to stand with men packed in like sardines in a tin. They would stand shoulder to shoulder when it was busy, but it did not matter if this caused a little inconvenience, everybody knew one another.

If a man were to take his wife into 'Black Jack's' they

would go into the parlour. Often he had marched along the street with his head held high like a soldier on parade, the only movement of his head would be to glance down at his shining shoes. After ordering a pint for himself, and a half pint for his missus, they would each take a sip just to get the taste buds active, then silence would cloud their thoughts and they would sit and stare ahead without so much as a word spoken to one another. So this was the start of a night out together, and the silence would only be broken when he decided to lift the pint glass from the table and put it to his lips, followed closely by his wife, with her half pint of Guinness, the creamy head still on it. Their lips would move in unison and their glasses would be put back on the table at precisely the same time.

The pattern was exactly the same for the other couples in the parlour, except for just those who had something to talk about due to the fact that they were a courting couple. All the other occupants of the room tried not to look at them by staring straight ahead or looking down at the floor, but in reality everybody was listening intensely to every word that the courting couple uttered.

By about nine-thirty in the evening, everybody would start chattering and their cheeks would start to flush, which was a sign that the tensions of life were gradually lifting from their shoulders. Talking would flow more freely, bringing an end to the formal silence. Conversation would now become spontaneous and the singing of songs passed down through the family would start, and those with passable voices would be asked to sing again. The parlour would now be full with not an empty seat, and nicotine would fall onto the glass on the bar counter before it was consumed.

One of the most striking things in 'Black Jack's', was the group of lonely old women who sat on wooden forms along the passageway of the pub. This passageway started at one door and went round at a forty-five degree angle to the next door, because the establishment was on the corner of the street. These old biddies were the last of an age that was, even then, speedily moving on. They had come out in the nineteenth-century and now they were old women in the early 1950s. They sat like clucking hens, clutching their glasses of stout, most of them with shawls around their shoulders to keep out the draught from the doors at either end of the passageway. I can never remember them wearing anything else other than long dark skirts, without a single ankle on view.

This I suppose also helped to keep out the chill wind that made its way along the passage every time somebody gained entrance. The women would sit on the long wooden forms without a speck of comfort but would be happy talking amongst themselves. They paid little heed to what went on either in the parlour at the back of them or the bar filled with men uttering some of the most vile obscenities; especially if it was on a Saturday night, when most of them had strong opinions as to the state of the local football results.

These elderly women sitting in the passage would never be lost for words and would constantly break into hilarious laughter. Most of them seemed to take snuff and would keep it in a small tin with a removable lid, or, if they had a son or husband who went away to sea, they could be in possession of a nice coloured snuff box that had been brought home for them. One of them would often offer a pinch of snuff to a man from the bar making his way to the toilet.

Smoking by women was frowned upon in public in that day and age. Many of them had never had a holiday in their lives and hardly moved more than a mile or so out of the area where they lived. Life was very harsh for them. They had few material possessions, but what they did have was dignity and strength of character.

To sit in 'Black Jack's' for a couple of hours once or twice a week was the reward for a lifetime of hard work. They had neither the time to have a nervous breakdown or the money to visit the doctor, except in absolute dire emergencies bordering on death. Most cures for their ailments had been passed down to them from parents who had been born long before the nineteenth century came to a close. Their shawls always seemed to be well-made and heavy, to keep at bay the cold and damp of the winter days, and the better shawls had shapely tassels hanging from them.

The women's hair was always tied at the back in a bun. They had helped to make the future yet they were from the past. They had come from the nineteenth century with the values of their youth, into a rapidly changing twentieth century, witnessing two world wars; but the changing new world had not really affected or changed them. Those stout-hearted, dignified women, sitting in a row along the passageway, had given birth to a generation, whose hopes for the future would, in the main, be counted by the material things in life; but those women were satisfied with only the bare necessities to keep them alive.

SMUDGE AND THE TWINS

Smudge was a handsome dog. He was a cross between an Alsatian and a mongrel, whose identity was never recorded; the size of a Labrador, with the build of a cocker spaniel, and the speed of a greyhound. His white coat and large black spots, combined with his long legs, made him stand out from all the other mongrel dogs in the area. He was also smart and cunning and was a favourite with the local kids. He was not a favourite with people on pushbikes or even those on motorbikes, as he would chase anyone who dared to pass him.

Smudge was also a bit of a coward as he would take great pleasure in chasing any dog that was smaller than himself, and when he came across one on a lead, it was his opportunity to show who was master. Big or small it never mattered, he knew he was on safe ground and they were unable to defend themselves. If they backed away Smudge would show them who was superior, and after frightening the life out of them he would walk away proudly down the road with his head up. If by chance the unsuspecting canine could defend him or herself, Smudge would sometimes take a beating which sent him skipping down the road with his tail between his legs, losing no time at all to gain the shelter of his home and his two companions, Billy and Johnny.

They were ten-year-old twins, tall for their age, each with a mop of blonde hair, blue eyes, and healthy bodies. Wherever the twins were found, Smudge was not too far away, as the three of them were inseparable. Their playground was mostly anywhere along the Dock Road and all streets running up from the docks, between the Pier Head, the Gladstone Dock and the Liverpool waterfront. The twins ran free like the wind, and Smudge was always by their side.

Billy and Johnny were two of five children, whose father had died three years earlier. Their mother could do little with them, as they were very self-assured, and would take little notice of her or anybody else for that matter, and certainly not the teachers in school. The boys were not cheeky, but appeared to be single-minded, and stayed away from school whenever the opportunity arose. Smudge was never on a lead and never wore a collar, as the twins held the belief that only pampered dogs had a collar and allowed themselves to be led about.

The two boys had a way with animals, which no other kids in the area had. If you gave them any animal you cared to choose, they could get it to perform some trick or other in a matter of minutes, but dogs were their favourite. On one occasion when the boys were out walking, Smudge walked into a butcher's shop and came running out with a big piece of steak in his jaws.

"Look at that daft canine," said Johnny.

"Don't you be swearin' at him, calling him a ca-nine," replied Billy.

"What de ya mean swearin'?" asked Johnny.

"Ya called him a ca-nine or something," Billy repeated.

"It was me Mam who called him a canine and she said that's what dogs are, they're canines," Johnny protested.

"Well I don't like ya callin' him by that name. Just call him Smudge like we always do."

"Alright, alright, have it your own way; I won't call him a canine again."

Smudge came running back to the boys after he had devoured the steak and he was still licking his mouth. He was not much younger than them and he loved being with them but he did, however, have one weakness. He was in love with an Alsatian, and she was not just any old mongrel, no, she was a police dog. Whenever he saw her, he would become so gentle, even making himself look foolish, rolling over on his back and making all sorts of daft noises.

Smudge was so enchanted with her that he would forget about the twins, and no amount of entreating would stop him from performing his peculiar courtship procedure. The twins and the policeman would be totally ignored by both animals and left looking on, as no amount of coaxing would drag Smudge from his lady love until his display was over. While Smudge was performing his ritual, the policeman would be laughing at him and the twins would be calling him such names as, "you're a stupid daft dog," and, "me Mam said we should have drowned you at birth, she's right, you daft dog."

It was only when the police dog got fed up with her admirer and turned her back on him, walking away without giving Smudge a backward glance, that he would come to his senses and go dashing down the road to catch up with the twins, who had always by then continued on their way and left him. When Smudge caught up with them, Billy turned to Johnny, "It's your fault he is like this, making a show of himself."

"No it's not," said an indignant Johnny. "He is in love and that's what happens when people or animals fall in love."

"But he is only a dog and me Dad said they don't fall in love," said Billy, determined to get the better of his brother.

"I know he is only a dog but me Mam said they can fall in love just like humans," was the reply.

So the argument went on until something else distracted their minds. School was not a priority with the twins but when they did go, their faithful dog would sit outside, no matter what the weather was like, waiting for his two friends to appear. At every chance they would sag school and the thought of being punished would never deter them. There were a lot of adventures out on the streets and that is where they always liked to be, running wild with Smudge.

The twins liked the school holidays best of all as they had the chance to go thieving. Robbing was what they had become good at and schoolwork only got in the way of taking what was not theirs. It was not as though the boys came from a dishonest family; their mother was a good woman with three younger children in addition to her extrovert ten year-old-twins.

Their father had died in tragic circumstances while working on the docks. After his death, the boys grew restless and wandered further away from home in their adventures with Smudge. He was supposed to sleep in the lobby under the stairs but most nights the twins would sneak him up to their room and he would lie at the bottom of their bed. Every morning when they were getting ready for school (that is if they had chosen to go to school, instead of 'sagging'), Smudge would be on the doorstep waiting to lead the way. Whether it was school or doing a 'bunk', Smudge would be out in front, running along the road like a greyhound,

Taking what was not theirs was part of the adventure of sagging school. It provided them with excitement, and they also earned respect from some of their school friends, and the chance to show off by displaying what they had stolen. Most of what they had taken would be cast to one side, such as throwing an old pair of boots in the bin; or they would swap them for a bag of sweets from an older more cunning school friend. The twins knew that they could get away with taking a bag of sweets home with them, but never with taking the proceeds of their day of adventure. The twins' mother was well aware of her boys running wild, so she was always on the look out to make sure they brought nothing into the house that did not belong to them.

Smudge would continue to lead the way, but would stop from time to time, sniffing the scent of some other animal who had gone before him. The boys would be hoping that the police dog would not appear, for fear of Smudge acting daft with his courtship nonsense. This always drew attention to them, and if they saw the police dog first, they would call Smudge and dodge down a side street to get him away from her. They liked nothing better than to walk along the Dock Road, sometimes casting an eye above the fence that circled the dock estate to see the masts and funnels of the ships using the port. Most of the time they would be looking into the warehouses and factories that ran the length of the road.

The twins had a plan of action which had been worked out to help them steal. They had trained Smudge to walk into a warehouse or any other establishment, and the dog would distract people by his friendliness, while the boys had a chance to look about and slip anything into their pockets that took their fancy. Smudge was such a capable and intelligent dog that they also taught him to stand on the pavement outside a building they had illegally entered after closing time, and Smudge would bark if anybody was passing.

They usually climbed in through a window that had not been securely fastened, or forced some other entry that presented few problems to the agile pair. On one occasion they had gone into a closed building as usual, leaving Smudge on guard duty outside. While the boys were blundering their way through a warehouse full of boxes of oranges, apples, and all sorts of exotic fruits from abroad, they felt a sense of excitement and adventure in what they were doing, safe in the knowledge that Smudge was keeping watch outside. The bottoms of their sweaters had been stuffed into their trousers and anything that the twins could gather went in at the neck, until their sweaters had ballooned out and they could no longer carry anymore.

They were like two pirates ripping open the fragile wooden boxes. Smudge had not given a warning bark so they slipped out of the front door of the building and walked out onto the pavement, only to find the dog laying on his back looking up into the eyes of the police dog and the policeman staring at their bulging sweaters.

"You must admit that dog of yours is pretty foolish when it comes to my Alsatian," said the policeman. "You two must be the prize idiots of all time to place your trust in such a silly dog. Anyway you're both nicked. Got the picture have you? Well, if you haven't, you soon will when the magistrate starts on you, to say nothing about what your mother is going to do to you both."

No one knew for sure what happened to the twins. They were never seen again on the Dock Road with Smudge leading the way looking for his favourite girlfriend.

THE YOUNG STARLING

A faint sound of an intermittent tiny squeak attracted the attention of the seven-year-old boy as he walked out from his mum's kitchen into the garden. It seemed to come from the direction of the sandstone encircling the rockery at the far end. The young boy's sharp hearing picked up the sound and where it came from. He put down the bowl full of breadcrumbs his mother had given him to feed the birds that landed in the garden because it was spring. She said they needed all the energy they could muster, as they were still caring for their young chicks.

William's shoes were making too much noise on the gravel path so he moved to the newly cut lawn and went onto his knees as he crept towards the rockery. He listened intensely in the hope of picking up the sound of the squawking again. Just at that moment a young bird with its flight feathers not fully formed, suddenly hopped from behind the rockery. William got a fright and jumped back, startled, then he became brave upon realising what had caused the noise and, still kneeling down in the grass, poked a finger at the young starling. Well, he thought it must be a starling because his mother kept pointing them out to him. When they landed in the garden, William's mother would say, "They're a nuisance those starlings, they come down covering the lawn and perch all along the fence." So he thought he had better not tell his mum in case she chased it away. As he pushed his finger towards the young bird, it moved its head back and opened its beak wide, the way it did when its mother was feeding it, but she was nowhere to be seen as William looked up into the tree.

He then tried reaching out to pick up the bird, but its nimble legs were too quick for him and it propelled itself across the lawn. Its young wings did not, as yet, have the strength to lift it off the grass, but it came to a sudden stop as though it had run out of energy. It was gasping for air and its little chest was pumping in and out like bellows, as the lack of nourishment seemed to be taking its toll. The young starling was not happy being so exposed on the open lawn, so it made its way between the thorny rose bushes. The boy tried in vain to reach into them but each time he caught the back of his hand on the thorns. William felt a stinging sensation, and let forth a blast of anger towards the young bird, as by this time it had moved further into the shelter of the bush.

William continued to rub the back of his hand as the pain came in waves.

"It's your fault I have to suffer," he shouted at the bird.

The young bird's response was to put its head back, open its beak and make a faint squeak, trying to summon its missing mother. Only the boy was responding to its distress call for help.

"Bloody nuisance," William cried out, still rubbing the back of his hand as he turned his back on the bird, and started to walk to the house.

He looked over his right shoulder towards the rose bushes, thinking to himself how ungrateful the young bird was. Then he stopped and turned once again towards it.

"I only wanted to rescue you, daft bird. You can stay there, and I hope the cats get you," he shouted as he continued his retreat into the house, still rubbing his hand.

Out in the garden the young starling was trying to attract attention by chirping and hopping about, but the lack of nourishment was now severe and soon the young bird came to a halt and sat still under the rose bush, exhausted of all energy.

Samson, the black cat from next door, had jumped up onto the six-foot fence and was walking along the top with perfect balance; his brain sending the right signals to every muscle in his body. Then the cat spotted the young starling but he was still in the rose bush. He brought himself to a rigid halt, his head protruding straight out from his shoulders, his keen vision locked onto his prey.

The young bird could see its predator but was either too immature or too weak to take evasive action and it simply sat in a hunched position with its head back. It seemed to be waiting for some divine presence, hopefully in the form of its mother landing alongside and grabbing it out of danger. This seemed to be in vain for only the cat was to be seen as it slowly edged forward, searching for the right spot to drop down into the garden. Samson heard the sound of the kitchen door open at the precise moment he sprang down, crouching in an attack position as the seven-year-old boy ran back into the garden.

William had by this time forgotten the pain in his hand and also the bird's presence as he tried to do handstands on the lawn, without much luck, because his legs kept falling back. He eventually gave up when he could not gain proper control of his legs. Samson still had one eye on William, as he crawled closer to the bird, preparing to pounce, when the lad started kicking at an imaginary ball. Samson was not to be outdone by this as he had plenty of patience and was prepared to bide his time. At last William lost interest in his games and headed for the house. Samson's eyes followed his departure from the garden, and then turned back to the helpless bird. Now he could strike.

The starling let out a faint squeak, which William's young ears picked up just as he was about to close the kitchen door. He turned towards the sound at the same moment as Samson sprang into action. His body was like a spring as the thrust of his back legs propelled him forward. William screamed at the top of his voice, reaching higher notes than a soprano, and charged towards the cat who, because of the sudden scream, had landed slightly to the side of the helpless bird, his claws missing it.

"Go away, go away, go away," screamed William.

Samson ran halfway up the garden, stopped, and looked back at the boy who had cheated him of his prey. The bird stood petrified, as his rescuer dropped to his knees and closed his small hand firmly, but gently around the starling.

"Got ya," he cried in delight.

The bird was silent as William got to his feet and looked up into the Hawthorn tree.

"I wonder where your mother is? Come on, me Mum will give you something to eat."

He made for the kitchen door, and the cat, who had jumped back onto the fence, sat glaring at him.

"What have you got in your hand?" said his mother as he walked into the kitchen. "Oh, I see it's a young bird. "Don't let go, I'll see if I can find something to put it in."

She produced a shoebox.

"Here, put it in this."

William gently lowered the bird down into the box. It flapped its wings in a vain bid to fly from captivity, but William placed his hand over the top to stop it getting away, and it gave up the struggle through exhaustion. Its beak wide open, the young bird sat waiting to be fed. The boy's mother placed two of her fingers into a glass of water, and then let the water drain from them, hoping some of it would drop into the open beak, but she had little success. The young bird would sooner have had its mother give it a nice juicy worm.

While William's mother tried to comfort the young

173

bird, he had been in the garden pulling up a handful of grass for the bird to lie on. He put the grass into the box, and then looked up at his mother.

"That will keep it warm," he said.

"You're quite right," she replied. "I know what we will do, we'll wet some little pieces of bread and perhaps it will eat that."

"Do you think it will, Mum?" asked William.

"Well we can try can't we?" she answered.

However this was all in vain again, as the young bird seemed unable to respond to the kindness of the boy's mother. William could see the concern on his mother's face for the captive.

"Do you think it will die, Mum?"

"No," she smiled, "we will think of something."

"I know, let's put it in the tree," William suggested.

"We can't do that, it will fall out, and then the cat will get it."

A sad look came over the boy's face.

"But it will die if we don't do something won't it?"

She looked at him not sure what to say, while her mind was searching for answers.

"I'm sure we will come up with the right idea," she continued, trying to comfort the seven-year-old.

"I've got it, Mum, let's put the shoe box in the tree just like a nest, then the bird can't fall out."

"Now that's a good idea," she said. "Here, you hold the box and I'll get the ladder out of the garden shed."

So off they went into the garden. William stayed at the bottom of the garden watching his mother return with a small ladder.

"This should get us up to the lower branches," she said, placing the ladder in position.

William spotted Samson sitting in the far corner of the garden, his eyes focused not on William but on the shoebox.

"Don't worry about him, he won't be able to reach the bird when we put it up into the tree," William's mother said as she started to climb up the ladder and William passed her the shoebox.

The young bird was silent as it slid about in the box.

"Don't drop it, Mum, that Samson is still watching."

His mother reached up into the tree to place the box between the trunk and a thick branch. When she was satisfied it was properly balanced, she looked to make sure the young bird was all right and then climbed down.

"Well, that's it, William, we can do no more," she sighed.

They both stood looking up into the tree as Samson, still crouching in the far corner in the garden, did the same. William's mum walked back to the shed with the ladder and William followed her, but then thought he would have one more look at the tree.

"Mum, Mum, look!" he shouted.

She turned around to see the young bird's mother standing on top of the box with a big, juicy worm in its beak. William and his mum were so pleased about this; but not so Samson, who was probably thinking about the prey that got away.

BORIS

He was a big fella, and very proud. You could tell that by the way he walked, his back straight, you could say rigid, his head held high; but it did nothing to impair the agility in his walk. Boris had a white coat with a touch of ginger around his head, which came down to encircle his right eye. His tail was mostly red with a few streaks of white. The tail was long and bushy and stood up like a skunk, but came down in a straight line with his body whenever he was stalking his prey, which could be anything from a bird to a mouse.

Boris was good at fending for himself. Tins of cat food were never on his menu when he was master of the back yard walls; such luxury was unheard of in his neck of the woods, well, back entries to be precise. Boris, like most felines was definitely his own master, but he also had to have a nice cosy fireside to come home to, especially after he had been out on a cold winter's night. On entering the house he would run his head and body across the legs of the first person he encountered, making sure of a warm welcome.

If Boris did have an enemy, it was the German Shepherd dog who lived next door. He was a big handsome fella with a long coat of fur that hung from his sides. His colour was fawn with black streaks, and generally he was a good-natured fellow, but his one weakness was that he did not like cats.

He never liked Boris from the first time he could scale the back yard walls when he was little more than a kitten. I imagine there was a fair bit of jealously on the part of the German Shepherd because he was confined to the small back yard and Boris was as free as a bird. I suppose it must have been hard on him having to walk up and down, and around in circles all day, bored out of his mind. When he saw a kitten walk along the wall and able to stroll wherever he wanted to, it must have driven him nearly insane.

Boris, like all kittens, was very playful and when he discovered that he could scale the walls for the first time, he would amble along the top of the wall goading the poor dog, while getting to know the neighbourhood. He would look the dog straight in the eyes, until the latter turned his back on Boris, breaking eye contact. He was becoming King of the back yard walls and, as the months went by, he had the pick of the female cats, as he was growing into a big handsome fellow.

This gave cause for a lot of bickering amongst the neighbourhood tomcats, so Boris was frequently attacked, but he was a match for any Tom who tried to encroach onto his territory. Boris had never paid a visit to the vet to patch up any of his war wounds. Nature was his vet, he just got on with life, with the exception of the time he broke his leg. Most of Boris's wounds were of a minor nature, but this one would keep him confined to the house for some time until the pain had subsided.

One morning, after a night on the tiles, it was clear to everybody that his front right leg was broken. Everyone in the household was concerned, running around not sure what to do, but eventually two flat pieces of wood were produced, a narrow bandage and a roll of plaster tape. Two pairs of hands held Boris down whilst the third person pulled his broken leg back into position, then the crude operation was completed by placing a flat piece of wood on each side of his leg, the bandage and plaster tape wrapped tightly around the crippled leg to make sure Boris would not be able to pull it away.

As the months went by Boris got stronger, and the German Shepherd became more frustrated watching the cat upon the wall enjoying life everyday, pleasing himself what he did. But perhaps the worst part was having to put up with Boris staring down at him continually, so the German Shepherd started to bark at Boris. However the barking had little or no effect on Boris as he would still continue to stare down at the dog, and he seemed to get great satisfaction from the poor German Shepherd becoming agitated by the constant eye contact.

Boris did not have a hate relationship with all canines. Living in the same household was a large dog called Buster who was the same colour as Boris, mostly white but with a coat that turned black when it got to the right side of his face giving the dog one white ear and the other black. Boris never took much notice of him although he was not a bad dog; well, he was good to Boris, and he would look after him when they were out in the street together. One source of enjoyment and freedom for Boris was trotting alongside Buster on the lead when out for a walk with his master. Boris, being almost the same colour as his pal, would cause a deal of amusement amongst the neighbours; the tall dog with his long legs and Boris running alongside him. No other dog would go near him when his canine friend was about. Not that Boris could not take care of himself, he was more than able for most predators that came his way.

During the summer months when the sun was shining, Boris had taken to lounging on the back wall, sometimes with his tail hanging down into the yard next door. It was one of those days when Boris was staring into the dog's eyes. The cat had sat down to enjoy the rays of the sun, his tail flicking up and down every time the flies, which always seemed to appear on warm days, had landed on his back. Boris started to dose off, unaware that the German Shepherd who was watching the tail, had slowly got to his feet from sitting position and made his way towards the wall that his tormentor was sleeping on.

The dog stood to his full height while looking up at the limp tail, and he never took his eyes from it as he went into a crouching position, his front legs pushing his weight against his back legs. When he had worked out the exact distance between himself and the tail, he gave one mighty push and sprung into action. He went up the wall like a pole vaulter, his strong jaws tightened around the tip of Boris's tail. He fell back onto his hind legs with satisfaction in his eyes as he looked up at his victim, who was making a terrible screeching noise while looking down into the eyes of his attacker.

The days and weeks went by and Boris's tail healed, but he never forgot what the German Shepherd dog had done to him. The cat still continued to goad the dog by standing on the wall and staring down at him, but every time Boris annoyed the dog, the latter would jump up the wall hoping to get to grips with his tormentor once again. But it was not to be. It was Boris who was on the offensive, waiting for the right time when he could strike back. He was back to his tricks again, walking up and down the wall, with the dog jumping up still trying to make contact. Boris, with his nose down towards the leaping dog, pushed his face down further without losing balance. Boris waited while the dog came even closer each time he leaped up the wall. Knowing he had to get his timing right, the German Shepherd leapt into action, his jaws open as he came up to meet the cat; but Boris struck first, his claw fully extended as it made contact like a cutlass, slicing through the tip of his nose. The dog was yelling and howling as it ran around the yard.

The weeks passed as the two combatants kept to their own territory, but in the course of time Boris eventually made his way down into the yard to sit alongside his old enemy; friends at last after so many battles.

THE STOWAWAYS

During the Second World War of 1939-1945, the only playground that many of the young and adventurous lads living near the docks in Liverpool had, was among the derelict buildings left by German bombing. They played in the air raid shelters, on the streets or in the empty houses that stood like skeletons without flesh. Their roofs and windows had been blown away, and houses that had once been homes to families, filled with laughter and tragedy, now seemed sad and lonely. Nearing the end of the war, many of the lads had reached their early teens and a group of them decided they would go on a great adventure.

"Who's goin'?" asked Hogger.

All the hands went up, representing five grubby thirteen and fourteen-year-olds. Yes, they were all keen to get away from the bombed houses that they had grown tired of playing in. They knew that if they stowed away on one of the big ships that sailed down the River Mersey, their lives would be full of adventure. They had heard this from the older boys and men who lived in their streets in Liverpool. The boys had often talked about other lads who had stowed away to sea. They had been told that when the Captain found them on the ship it would be well out into the ocean and he would sign them on as members of the crew.

"The only thing we need now is a ship," said Hogger Smith.

Hogger was the leader of the gang. He was fourteen-and-a-half and worked on the docks as a can-lad and it was not everyone who could make a good brew of tea. If he did a good job of this, the men would appreciate it and they would make his life that much easier, by not giving him the worst jobs such as hanging over the ship's side, scraping off rust.

Andy Doyle was number two, by virtue of the fact that his Dad was still at sea and was a ship's Bosun. Some of the lads said that meant he was a Petty Officer. Joey Collins was number three. Two of his brothers were seamen, but they were only Able Seamen, not like Andy's Dad.

Mickey Mullens was next in line. Now Mickey was a good thief and had never been caught stealing from bombed-out buildings, so he would know how to find food for them if this was needed. Then there was the quiet member of the gang, Sunny Nelson. He was cunning and smart and would always have any problems worked out while the rest of them were still counting on their fingers.

"It's not the ship we should be worrying about at this stage, it's getting past the copper on the dock gate," said Sunny.

"No problem, I know where there's a loose board in the fence," said Hogger.

"When are we goin'," asked Mickey Mullens.

"What d'yer say we go tomorra night?" replied Hogger.

Not a word was spoken as they stood in silence.

"Right then, see ya all at the top of Haddick Street at seven o'clock tomorra night," said Hogger.

The appointed time came and they were all prepared, without a penny in their pockets, though not that many of them had pockets in their trousers. Three of them had pumps on, one had boots and the fifth, Andy Doyle, had shoes. They had no overcoats to protect them from the cold winter nights, and no caps to stop the rain from beating on their heads.

Hogger surveyed his band of would-be sailors, who

were all ready for the great adventure that lay ahead. They did not believe in wasting time preparing for this expedition. From its inception, right up to the hour that their plans would be put into operation, it took only twenty-four hours. No one could accuse them of not being men of action, even though they were only thirteen and fourteen.

Hogger and his little gang had lived with the violence that fell from the sky, but now the war was almost over their education was complete. They walked through the dock estate in the darkness of the cold November night in 1944, with piercing eyes searching for the ship of their dreams. Hogger and his gang seemed like five young players floating across the stage. All the lights on the dock estate had been removed because of the war, but that would not deter the young adventurers. They had walked around for some hours during the early evening, in search of the right ship. Any old ship that lay tied up, still discharging its cargo was not considered. The intelligence work was provided by Hogger and Andy Doyle, for were they not steeped in the knowledge of ships?

The five continued to walk in silence, except for Joey's squeaking boots, towards the bridge which would take them to the west side of the docks alongside the River Mersey. They heard voices coming out of the inky darkness, from the direction of the bridge, then a light showed up the doorway of the dock gateman's hut on the far side of the bridge. The voices and the light were soon gone and the lads were cast into darkness and silence once again.

"Can't go over the bridge now," said Hogger.

"If they come out of the hut we've 'ad it," one of them replied.

"No need to worry," said Sunny Nelson, who was one step ahead of his pals. "I've found a pontoon, and if we get a few pieces of wood we can row across like we do on the canal, when we make a raft."

This experience came in handy as they climbed down the ladder that was secured to the dock wall by a rope. With their piece of wood at the ready to be used as an oar, they set off into the darkness to get to the other side in their flat-bottomed-pontoon. The craft was used for cleaning and painting ships when they were in port, but this was no pleasure boat. It was coated in oil, paint and grease, but who worried about a little discomfort when on such a great adventure? The night was still dark, except for the distant stars. The crescent moon was also in the sky and could just about be seen with the naked eye. The docks were without lights, to keep any approaching enemy at bay, but the adventurers were glad of the inky darkness. Sonny Nelson's mind started to run away with him.

"If only we were commandoes, just think what we could do with the enemy. We could sail across the sea and surprise 'em. Then shoot 'em in their sleep and sail away into the darkness and the next morning, when it was light, a big ship would see us and the Captain would be so pleased with what we had done, he would sign us all on. Then we would be part of the crew."

"Come on, Nello," said Hogger.

He always called him Nello when he was annoyed with him. "You're standing like someone in a trance. Pick that piece of wood up and start to row."

Hogger gave the orders and stood like the boy on the burning deck, except that this was a greasy, moving deck. Every time Joey stirred, his boots would squeak because he would be pulling them one way while the paint and grease tugged him the other way.

"Keep them boots quiet," demanded Andy Doyle, just like the First Mate on a big ship, with Hogger as the Captain and Andy the First Officer. The makeshift oars were slapping against the stinking water of the dock and the pontoon was making for the far side. Its crew fell silent with the fear of the unknown. Every time they moved their feet, the filth and wet paint from the deck would cling to their footwear. Fear started to grip the adventurers, and it seemed like an eternity before the pontoon hit the far wall of the dock.

Hogger marshalled his ragged, cold and hungry troops.

"We have to get some food," said Sonny Nelson.

"Let's look for a canteen," suggested Mickey Mullens.

"But they're all closed," replied Joey.

"Of course they're all closed, so we will have to break in," said Mickey.

They eventually found what they were looking for and after gaining entrance, Mickey wanted to go further into the kitchen storeroom, but his little gang refused, as breaking the window to get in was the only damage they wanted to do. So dry toast it had to be, leaving the boys cold and still hungry, fearing footsteps in the dark, in case it was a policeman.

Sunny Nelson had been given the task of finding the right ship. It had to be one making ready for sea.

"That looks like the right one," suggested Sonny.

"It's a big ship," added Mickey.

"It's taking on cargo," said Hogger.

"Yes, and I can see a guard at the top of the gangway," said Andy.

"We can't go on board until the guard goes away," grumbled Joey, his boots still squeaking each time he moved.

"If you don't stop them boots from squeakin' everybody on the ship will hear us," ordered Hogger.

Sunny Nelson went on another scouting mission, closer to the ship and watched the guard leave his post at the top of the gangway. "Come on lads, he's gone," said

Sunny to the young men of action. They all jumped down from the bales of cotton that they had been lying on in the dock shed.

Hogger gave his orders, "Come on lads, let's get up the gangway before the guard comes back."

Once on board they found a lifeboat with a canvas cover.

"This will do us," said Hogger and they piled in.

Hours went by and the dawn broke through with the sounds of footsteps, laughter and men talking.

"Wish I 'ad a cigarette," grumbled Mickey.

"Have a look outside, see who's there," asked Joey.

"It's soldiers," replied Mickey, "Hundreds an' hundreds of them."

"It must be a troop ship," added Hogger.

"I'm goin' to ask them soldiers for a fag," said Andy.

"Yer can't," replied Sunny Nelson, "they will tell the Captain."

"No they won't," said Hogger, "I need a fag too."

"Eh, mate, have ya got a fag," asked Andy, pulling the canvas back to show the pathetic little band of would-be adventurers.

A group of soldiers looked in amazement at the boys, filthy and dishevelled, huddling together in the lifeboat. One soldier stepped forward and gave Andy a cigarette and he struck a match for him to light up. The rest of them seemed to be looking in disbelief at the scene before them as their heads disappeared once again under the canvas of the lifeboat.

"What did I tell yer. They'll never tell the Captain," said Andy, sitting in a cloud of smoke under the canvas.

For all the bravado, the lads were beginning to feel the cold as they crouched down, and hunger was starting to take its toll on the five of them. About ten minutes after Andy's cigarette was extinguished there was an unnatural silence from the soldiers as their laughter and banter ceased on the open deck of the ship. Hogger decided he had better investigate what was happening when, without warning, the canvas was pulled back by members of the crew, exposing Hogger and his little band of would-be adventurers, who discovered they had just spent a cold night on board a ship not due to sail for another twenty-four hours.

Embarrassed and dejected, the lads stood in line on the deck as the young soldiers tried not to laugh at them. Smiling pitifully, they looked in amazement at the lads, who were marched up to the police station to face the Police Sergeant who was on duty. When the Sergeant looked at the lads he had to stop himself from laughing so that he could give them a dressing down and try and explain to them the anguish they had brought to their families. Hogger's father was sent for to collect all of them. Just a few years later, three had their wish come true and became merchant seamen, while Mickey Mullens finished up in the Irish Guards and Sunny Nelson joined the Royal Navy.

THE STUDENT

She sat cradling her textbooks like a mother holding her baby close to her breast while she gently patted its back. Jackie looked more like a girl of sixteen than the nineteen-year-old English Literature student who has wandered into the sitting room of the old Victorian house, where she shared a bedsit with two other students. Her movements took up a rocking motion as she pulled the books closer to her whilst she watched the television. She did not appear to notice any other person in the room, as she gave a running commentary on the programme she was watching. No one in the room interrupted her, for her words seemed so personal; not really meant for the ears of others.

"I don't suppose they will show Fermanagh; it's a lovely County. But, of course I'm bound to say that," said Jackie.

"Enniskillin – it would be nice to see on the television," Jackie's eyes were fixed on the black and white screen.

Far nicer if it was in colour, she thought to herself.

The camera picked up a small boat. A gentle breeze was lifting the bow of the small craft, but not enough to disturb the man who was the sole occupant of the tiny craft.

"The waters are blue, you know."

Nobody answered in case they altered the flow of Jackie's observations.

"Well, it could be the blue waters of Lough Erne."

The room was silent except for her speaking; the only other sound was from the television commentator. She was listening to him describing a world she knew –

although she had not explored so much of the North.

"The divisions – the divided people – it's my people they are talking about."

Her thoughts still flowed for all to hear and the man in the small craft kept on fishing in the gentle breeze on the peaceful lough.

Opening wide, Jackie's eyes tried to hold back the tears.

"Have you ever been to Fermanagh; it is a lovely part of the world?"

The textbooks were clutched tighter, whilst Jackie's feelings and recollections came flowing out.

"It doesn't have to be like that; my country and our people divided. My family work hard. My father died too young, working the land to feed us."

The fisherman in his boat returned to the screen.

"My father used to fish in the lough. He was a good man, never hurt anyone."

Everyone just sat and listened, not daring to utter a word. A little sniff and a ray of light shot across Jackie's eyes.

"It's good to see a programme about Ireland, showing us as a people who have a love of nature. We are part of that nature; we have lived and worked the land for thousands of years. Our entire culture evolved from the land; our legends, our mythology were given meaning from the land."

Jackie paused, as though waiting for a response from her friends who sat in silence not wanting to disrupt her stream of thought.

"We are good people. Nice to see the countryside instead of the tragedies of urban city life. With a little luck, we may see the village I come from, Tempo. Yes, and Enniskillin – a lovely little town."

The images came to the screen and Jackie saw the

lough and green villages back down the passage of time to her childhood; a childhood knowing no peace; walking past men with strange uniforms, driving ugly vehicles, as though they were in a sinister part of a lovely landscape. The man in the boat appeared once again on the screen.

"It could be lower Lough Erne," said Jackie with a gentle rocking motion from her body, with her textbooks still clutched to her bosom, her eyes and mind still held by the mirror that was a television screen, producing the images she longed to see.

The pain of the last few months came to the surface of her being, like it had been exorcised from her; memories of an evil landlady being spirited away, as she watched her lovely Fermanagh. Jackie let go of the bad experiences of her former landlady; a woman who had given the second year student a hard time in her first taste of private accommodation since she had left Fermanagh. Jackie's student friend had tried to protect her from the cruel remarks made by the landlady with the viper's tongue.

"Go back to Ireland, you Irish bastard. You're all the same," she would scream each time the television newsreader gave a bad press about Ireland.

She would bang on the door, "You're all the same," screeching at the five-foot-nothing Jackie through the thin panels of the door.

The commentary from the documentary kept Jackie's attention – a copy of Seamus Heaney's *North*, lying on top of the rest of the textbooks.

"I wonder what she would say if she was watching this programme?" said Jackie.

Her gaze moved from the television screen and she smiled.

"I bet the old witch would still have some adverse comment to make."

Jackie's fellow lodgers smiled back, but made no comment; it was unlike Jackie to make snide remarks, even about people as vile as her previous landlady.

"Yes, that's my homeland; it's lovely isn't it?"

Her face had become radiant. The rocking motion had stopped, her back straightened; her whole being seemed free from the months of torment. She knew that she was among friends at last; friends with whom she could express her innermost feelings.

The room became silent, as the programme came to an end, and Jackie recalled a fragment of a poem: "This refuge offers continuity; A growing where you will know The changing of season."

Jackie stood up, still clutching her books. She smiled at her friends with a mixture of embarrassment and satisfaction and then left the room.